HOW TO AVOID A SCANDAL (OR NOT)

MERRY FARMER

HOW TO AVOID A SCANDAL (OR NOT)

Copyright ©2021 by Merry Farmer

Cover design by Erin Dameron-Hill (the miracle-worker)

ASIN: B09DLFNN25

Paperback ISBN: 9798464386129

Click here for a complete list of other works by Merry Farmer.

If you'd like to be the first to learn about when the next books in the series come out and more, please sign up for my newsletter here: http://eepurl.com/RQ-KX

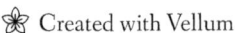 Created with Vellum

CHAPTER 1

LONDON – MAY, 1888

She hated him. Lady Diana Pickwick hated Lord John Darrow, Viscount Whitlock, with the fire of a thousand suns. She hated him when she woke up in the morning, as she went about her business during the day, paying calls and attending to the various political causes the May Flowers championed, and she hated him when she went to bed at night.

He was standing across the large salon the May Flowers had rented for their political rally and tableau of powerful women in history, looking as smug as you please in his expertly tailored suit. The fashionable lines of the jacket accented John's broad shoulders and trim waist. The way he moved as he laughed over something one of his friends said showed off the power in his fine frame. His dark eyes danced with mischief, and he brushed a hand through his thick, chestnut locks as he composed himself after his laughter. The strong set of his jaw formed a perfect contrast to his sensual lips.

Not that Diana noticed any of that. She cleared her throat and dragged her eyes back to the podium she was arranging for the day's speeches. She hated John Darrow. He was a menace and a rogue. He'd teased her mercilessly for over two years now, always singling her out for pranks and games at the gatherings their friends held. He winked at her and flirted with her, whether she wanted it or not, even in public. He vexed her at every turn, treating her the way a man would treat a barmaid at his favorite pub instead of taking her seriously. She was the leader of the May Flowers, after all. She had a right to be treated with respect. Something John failed to do in even the smallest way with his flashing eyes and his expressive mouth and his—

"Good heavens, Diana. If you keep staring at the man like that, you're likely to cause his clothes to combust and fall right off of him," Lady Bianca Clerkenwell said, startling Diana out of her thoughts.

"I beg your pardon?" she asked, her voice coming out breathless and strangled. She hadn't heard Bianca approach, hadn't noticed her sister, Natalia Townsend, with her, and likely wouldn't have noticed if the roof had caved in, raining puppies on them all.

Bianca grinned knowingly, patting Diana's arm with a look of mock sympathy. "There, there," she said, barely keeping her laughter—or her ribald sense of humor—in check. "If you want to lure the man into marriage, all you need to do is follow those sultry looks with sultry actions."

"I do not—how could you suggest—John Darrow is the last man on earth that I would want to take tea with, let alone marry," Diana snapped. She might have stomped her foot as she avowed it as well.

Bianca and Natalia exchanged an amused look, their eyes sparkling with mirth.

"Marriage is actually quite lovely," Natalia said. "Linus and I enjoy it very much."

"And heaven knows Jack and I are fond of the institution," Bianca added. She smoothed a hand over her stomach. "Perhaps a little too fond."

Natalia whipped to face her. "Again?"

Bianca sent her sister a sheepish look. "As if you're one to talk."

Natalia sucked in a breath, her eyes going wide. "You aren't supposed to know about that yet," she whispered.

"Darling, it's written all over your face," Bianca said.

Their conversation was interrupted as Diana's closest friend, Lady Beatrice Manfred, skipped over to join them by the podium. Bea practically glowed with excitement, her cheeks rosy and her eyes bright. Diana instantly dreaded what could have put such joy on Bea's face.

"I'm so happy to have found you all here," Bea said, grabbing Diana's arm and giggling. "I wanted you all, my dearest friends, to be the first to know." She, too, dropped a hand to her stomach.

"No." Diana shook her head, peeling Bea's hand away from her arm. "No, I refuse to hear it. Not you too."

"Me too?" Bea blinked, her mirth turning to confusion.

Bianca raised one hand with a laugh. "It seems Natalia and I are in good company."

Bea's smile returned full force. "The two of you as well?"

Natalia grasped Bea's hand and giggled. "Do you suppose all three of us will give birth in the same month? Oh, how lovely to think our children will all be of an age and grow up together! Perhaps, if one is a boy and another is a girl, they might even marry someday."

That was the final straw, as far as Diana was concerned. No, the final straw was when she glanced across the room as a means to escape her friends' joy and found John staring right at her with that wicked little grin of his. As if he knew what sort of news her friends were sharing. As if he wanted to make it four pregnancies instead of three. How dare the bastard grin at her so blatantly in public? He made her feel so...so...so....

She huffed out a breath and turned back to her friends. "Many felicitations on your happy conditions," she said in clipped tones. "Now, if you will excuse me, some of us have chosen to continue the fight for the rights of women rather than sliding into tired old patterns of motherhood."

Diana knew the moment the words were past her lips that she sounded peevish and bitter. Her friends didn't deserve that. Fortunately—or perhaps very much unfortunately—all three of them looked at her with sympathy and understanding.

"Your time will come soon, darling. Just you wait," Bianca said.

"You sound exactly like my mother," Diana growled. "Don't let her hear you talking."

"Is she here?" Bianca glanced around.

"She is, and Papa too," Diana sighed. "As though I am a child giving a recital that they have to attend."

"Then I'll just go have a word with them and suggest ways they can make your time come sooner," Bianca teased her.

"I do not want my time to come at all," Diana insisted in reply. "I have only ever had one aim in life, and that is to be a strong, independent, powerful woman, like the women we will be portraying in today's tableau."

"Yes, I suppose we should all don our costumes for that," Bea said. "It's too early for any of the audience to know they are watching three women in a delicate condition."

"At least three," Natalia said. "I heard that Cynthia Withers is expecting as well."

"Oh?" Bianca raised one eyebrow, sending a concerned look Diana's way. She slipped her arm around her sister's back and gently led her to the curtain that separated the area where the podium stood from the backstage area, where the tableau was being set up. "Do tell me all about it."

Diana watched them go, doing her best to maintain an air of strength and fortitude. One final look of compassion from Bea before she, too, slipped backstage had Diana's heart sagging. She fussed with the notes for her speech that sat on the podium, trying to chase the gloom from her heart.

She was the last of her friends who remained unmarried. In the past few years, she'd watched each of them—from Cecelia Marlowe years ago to Bea just a few months prior—walk down the aisle to marry good men. Even Freddy Harrington and Reese Howsden had discreetly taken up with each other and were now raising a foundling girl, along with Reese's son, Harry, though she wasn't supposed to know the scandalous truth of their romance. It all made Diana feel very much like a dusty old doll that had been put on a back shelf, never to be played with again. She was hard-pressed to find men who would so much as waltz with her when she attended balls anymore, let alone ones who would walk out with her.

Not that she wanted to walk out with any man.

She shot a look straight across the room to John, her eyes narrowing. It was all John's fault. He monopolized her time, both in public and in private. How was she supposed to draw the attention of anyone else when he constantly loomed over her the way he did? It wasn't as though he had any intentions toward her other than his attempts to drive her mad.

Her heart thudded miserably over that thought in a way that felt distinctly like yearning.

No, that was wrong. She did not want John Darrow. She did not want him in any way at all.

She cleared her throat and called out, "Ladies and gentlemen! Ladies and gentlemen, please give me the honor of your attention."

The room quieted with surprising speed. Diana had always possessed a powerful voice that demanded people listen to her. She wasn't ignorant of the way her striking beauty held attention either. But if she was so very beautiful, why was she the last of her friends to snag a husband?

She instantly pushed that thought aside with a bout of fury at herself. At least that fury was useful when it came to expounding on the cause that meant so much to her.

"Ladies and gentlemen, we are here today to celebrate the strength and power of women throughout the ages," she began, standing tall and meeting the eyes of as many of the men and women in her audience as she could. When she met John's eyes as he stared at her with a grin, arms crossed, she tilted her chin up farther and went on. "You all know that the goal of the May Flowers is to fight for women's right to vote. The right to have our

7

voice heard and to have our opinions counted in matters of government is exceedingly important. For it is our leaders that decide our fates. To be denied the right to have a say in who those leaders are is scandalous.

"But I want to speak to you today about something that I believe is equally as important," she went on, shifting to grip the edges of the podium. She stared particularly at the women in the audience as she said, "Ladies, though it is not a topic we are encouraged to think of, each and every one of you should turn your attention to your financial independence."

A surprised murmur passed through the room. It was precisely the sort of reaction Diana had expected for her unusual topic.

"That is right, my friends," she continued. "Several years ago, in eighteen eighty-two, our allies in Parliament passed the Married Women's Property Act. Among other things, this forward-thinking parliamentary measure has given us the right to conduct our business as our own. We no longer need the permission or the supervision of our husbands, fathers, or brothers to maintain and grow our own finances. Our income does not automatically become the property of our husbands when we marry, and I, for one, think it is essential that we make the most of that."

Judging by the mutters and hums of the audience, Diana would have thought she'd called for a revolution. She loved the zip of tension her suggestion brought with it, though, so she went on with enthusiasm.

"Now is the time, ladies, to educate yourselves about matters of money and investments. Now is the time to search out financial opportunities and to increase your own bank accounts. Women should no longer be reliant on pin money provided to us by the men in our lives. For the first time ever, we have it within our power to support ourselves on our own income. I believe this is the single most important step a woman can take to secure herself and her future. It is not the pen that is mightier than the sword, it is the pound."

She finished her speech with a triumphant smile and was rewarded with enthusiastic applause from many of the ladies present. The applause from the rest of the room was somewhat less enthusiastic, and a few of the gentlemen in attendance looked downright offended. Diana sought out John to see what he thought, but the blighter was already in conversation with his friends, Bea's husband, Harrison, and Freddy and Reese. Diana tried not to take it personally, but it stung that he wasn't paying attention to her.

No, that wasn't right. She didn't give a fig what John Darrow thought of her.

"And now," she went on, "in a few moments' time, the ladies of the May Flowers would like to present to you our tableau of powerful women throughout history."

A renewed smattering of applause followed as Diana stepped away from the podium and headed backstage. She needed to change into her costume depicting the Greek goddess Athena as quickly as possible, as she was

9

one of the first scenes in the tableau. As pleased as she'd been with her idea earlier, it felt hollow now. She was filled with brave words about how women should live their lives—and her own financial portfolio was an impressive example of living up to her words—but more often than not, she felt as though she were fighting a losing battle against forces that hadn't changed for hundreds of years and wouldn't change anytime soon.

JOHN ADORED HER. LADY DIANA PICKWICK WAS simply the most delightful creature God had ever made. Watching her speak, observing the way she held her audience captive with her beauty and her wit, never failed to stir his blood in his veins. As far as John was concerned, there wasn't a lovelier and more exciting woman in all of creation. She was elegance and wisdom personified. He loved everything about her, from her perfect shape to her sharp mind. He wasn't going to pretend he was anything other than a red-blooded male by ignoring her pert breasts or her kissable mouth either. In short, Diana was perfection.

"If you looked any more like a lovesick schoolboy, we'd force you to wear short pants and to go bed without supper," Harrison laughed, slapping John's back as he watched Diana sweep backstage for her tableau.

"I look perfectly reasonable," John argued. "A man can adore a woman without making a fool of himself."

The others laughed. "Since when has that ever been

true?" Reese asked, exchanging a knowing grin with Freddy.

John laughed along with them. Reese and Freddy had behaved like perfect sots around each other. At least, they had when they could get away with it. And Harrison had made a complete ass of himself at Christmas in his attempts to propose to Lady Bea.

"There is nothing wrong with my behavior where Lady Diana is concerned," John said.

His friends snorted and shook their heads in disbelief.

"You're horrible to her," Harrison pointed out. "You flirt and tease her, then leave her hanging."

"Unless there's more that you haven't told us," Freddy said, one eyebrow raised.

A paradoxical sort of sadness filled John's chest. If only there were more to the situation than his friends knew. Many had been the times in the last two years when he'd seriously considered seducing Diana like a cad. He drove himself to distraction on a regular basis imagining how amazing it would be to bed her. She would be a firebrand in bed, he was certain. He could barely contain himself at the thought of her naked body splayed beneath him. He could practically hear the sounds she would make as he pleasured her. His imagination ran wild almost nightly, but all he had to satisfy himself was his own hand.

"There isn't anything I haven't told you," he said to his friends with a sigh, adjusting the way he stood to hide what his thoughts were doing to him. "And unless certain situations change soon, there won't be anything else."

All three of his friends stared at him with frowns.

"This doesn't have anything to do with that canal investment, does it?" Harrison asked, his frown turning scolding.

John felt his face heat. He glanced away for a moment, hoping his friends wouldn't see the shame in his eyes. "It was an unmitigated disaster," he admitted in a quiet voice. "So was the investment in that gold mine in South Africa. And the shipping contract I was told would mean guaranteed wealth."

"How many faulty investments does that make now?" Reese asked, compassion in his expression.

The compassion made John squirm. "Too many," he admitted in a mumble.

An awkward silence fell. Freddy, Harrison, and Reese shared another round of sage looks.

At last, Reese cleared his throat and said, "You know what men have done for centuries when their financial situations have become untenable, don't you?"

John's face heated even more. "Sought employment?" he answered, knowing that wasn't what Reese had in mind.

"They've married a woman with a fat dowry or money of her own," Reese said exactly what John knew he would. Reese nodded to the stage area at the front of the room. It had been cleared, but Diana's presence still somehow loomed large. "You heard what Diana said. I'd wager she has a nest egg of her own you might avail your-self of."

"No," John answered so quickly and vehemently that a pair of middle-aged ladies beside them stopped their conversation to stare at John. They clucked and shook their heads at his rudeness. When they returned to their conversation, John lowered his voice and said to his friends, "No. I'm not going to hoist my problems off onto Diana. I dug this hole for myself and I will find a way out of it myself."

Harrison shifted, studying John as if seeing him anew. "Is this why you haven't proposed to Diana already?"

"Don't tell me you've left the poor woman hanging all these years because of money," Freddy added.

John's shoulders slumped. He hated the way his foolishness made him feel. He only allowed himself to slump for a moment before clearing his throat and standing straighter. "I have held off on asking Diana to marry me because it would be a crime to enter a marriage without the financial means to support any woman in the way she deserves."

"But you're a bloody viscount, man," Freddy argued.

"And as you well know, Freddy, having a title doesn't mean anything when the estate attached to it has been steadily failing for years," John shot back.

It was a low blow, and Freddy colored in reaction to it. Freddy himself had inherited a bankrupt estate and nearly lost it. Reese had come to his rescue by purchasing

the land and the debt associated with Freddy's inheri-
tance, but as John understood it, the move had almost
driven a wedge between them permanently. He would
rather have died than disappoint Diana in a similar
manner.

"You need to talk to her about this," Reese said with
his unique blend of command and caring. "You need to at
least tell her the reason you haven't proposed is because
you're not in a financial position to do so."

"It would be a damn sight better than continuing to
vex the poor woman the way you do," Harrison went on.

"But vexing her is so much fun," John said with a
renewed sense of cheer. "The woman is a delightful little
minx when she has her back up."

"Yes, but getting a woman's back up isn't nearly as
much fun as getting her on her back," Harrison replied
with a smirk.

John let out a breath. He wasn't going to win the
argument and he knew it. Still, he wasn't sure he could
let go of his pride by confessing. His pride was the only
thing he had left, and it was precious to him.

"I'll go speak to her," he said with a sigh.

"Do it right now," Harrison insisted, shifting so that
he could push John toward the stage area. "Do it while
you still have the nerve."

"And while your friends are holding you account-
able," Freddy said.

John gave them all withering looks, but he stepped
forward as he did. They had a point. Diana deserved the

truth. And it would be far easier to deliver it, knowing his friends were nearby and that they would never let him hear the end of it if he backed down from the challenge. There was nothing for it but to soldier on, to charge forward, and to humiliate himself in front of the woman he loved by admitting what a failure he was.

CHAPTER 2

*T*he stage—or what passed for one in the rented hall—was set, and most of the ladies of the May Flowers who had volunteered to portray the great ladies of history for the tableau were in place. Diana had very little left to do before their performance began. Lady Henrietta O'Shea was already in place near the split in the center curtain, script in hand, ready to walk out and narrate the spectacle. Diana considered it a stroke of luck that they'd been able to secure Henrietta's services. She was the former leader of the May Flowers, but she'd bowed out after marrying Lord Fergus O'Shea and becoming embroiled in a bit of a scandal. She and Fergus were about to depart for Fergus's holdings in Ireland, and it was whispered that they wouldn't return for years, as they intended to raise a family in Fergus's homeland.

Diana huffed with impatience and adjusted the folds of her Greek costume. Yet another of her friends who was disappearing into domestic life. Frustration pinched her face, but gloom invaded her heart. Both emotions made her feel like a ninny, so she fought to push them aside.

"Are we nearly ready?" she whispered to Henrietta.

Henrietta pivoted to check with the rest of the ladies on the far side of the stage, then turned back to Diana. "A few more minutes, I think," she said. "Bianca is still fussing with her Boadicea armor."

The corner of Diana's mouth ticked up, though whether in amusement or impatience she couldn't tell. She questioned her decision to cast Bianca in the role of the powerful, medieval warrior. She questioned the wisdom of putting together a tableau at all.

Tableaux had become all the rage in women's circles of late. They were simple to execute and engaging to stage. All they required were elaborate sets and costumes to illustrate a story from history or literature. The participants dressed in fancy costumes, struck a pose on the set, and held that pose while a narrator described the scene. Tableaux also had the advantage of allowing women to dress in a manner they never would have been able to get away with under other circumstances. Diana's loose, flowing Greek costume was a perfect example. It left her creamy shoulders bare and accented her shape in a way that even the most structured corset didn't. And why shouldn't she show off her form? Part of the movement for the rights of women that she championed so loudly was for women to be able to dress in comfort in a way that improved their health instead of strangling them.

"Almost there," Henrietta whispered across to her. The audience on the other side of the curtain was growing restless and chattering loudly. "Millicent can't find her wig for Queen Elizabeth."

Diana huffed impatiently and stared at the curtain in front of her, feeling as though they would never get started. "Should we go ahead without her? We have three sections of the stage."

"Not unless you want Millicent to strike you from the list of every social event she has planned," Henrietta warned.

Diana scowled, ready to burst. They could have begun. The way the tableau was arranged, the stage was divided into three sections. Each section would open independently, allowing the other two to be switched about while one was the focus of attention. The center section would open first with Natalia portraying the judge Deborah from the Bible. Then they would move on to Diana's Athena. If they could just get started with the first scene, they would—

Her thoughts were cut short and she gasped as none other than John parted the curtain in front of her and stepped into her stage area. John flinched as hard as she did as he let the curtain drop behind him.

"Do you always lurk behind curtains, waiting to frighten a man out of his wits like that?" he asked, color splashing his handsome face and accenting his wicked grin.

"I wasn't aware that you had any wits to scare out," she replied, crossing her arms.

The effect of her gesture wasn't what she'd anticipated. Without her usual conservative clothing, crossing her arms only served to thrust her breasts up. John's gaze dropped immediately to drink in the sight, and his eyes lit with unabashed appreciation. Diana debated moving her arms and assuming a more modest posture, but sheer stubbornness prevented her.

"What do you want, John?" she asked in a flat voice that demanded he look up at her rather than drooling over her breasts.

John was incredibly slow to raise his head and grin at her. "You, Diana. You in all of your peevish, impossible glory."

Diana's heart fluttered in her chest, and she nearly dropped her arms to her side and leaned toward him.

Until he said, "Or at least you and those remarkable orbs of yours displayed invitingly in my bed."

Diana let out a sound of disgust, fighting against the tightening of her nipples and the ache that formed in her sex. "You are an ugly lout, John Darrow." She sniffed, tilting her head up. "I knew you were a reprobate, but I had no idea you were so vulgar."

"I'm sorry, Diana, sweeting," he apologized in an overly sweet voice, inching closer to her. "But you are irresistible, you know."

"I am nothing of the sort," she insisted. He was merely teasing her, as usual. The mocking in his eyes and the twitch of his luscious mouth said as much. If he were serious about the way he wanted her, he would have done something about it ages ago.

"My, my. With a frosty attitude such as that, you'd think you were portraying your namesake, the virgin goddess Diana, instead of Athena."

Diana's face burned hot at his use of the word "virgin". It was the very last thing she wanted to be, but it seemed to be her fate.

"I repeat. What do you want, John?" she snapped, wishing there were a way to calm the raging in her heart.

He shifted, taking in the sight of her, the mood radiating from him changing slightly. A more serious look came to his eyes. "I wanted to...." He shifted again, pressing his lips tightly together. "I think the time has come...." Again, he paused. He rubbed a hand over his face. "Circumstances are such as...."

Diana sighed tersely. "Whatever you have to say, John, say it. The tableau is about to start."

She glanced to Henrietta, but her friend had moved to the far end of the stage. Millicent stood in the center of a circle of other participants, looking as though she didn't know how to make heads or tails of her Elizabethan costume.

"It's about your speech," John rushed on, pulling Diana's attention back to him. "You see, the thing about money is...." Diana clenched her jaw and stared sharply at him. Surprisingly, John looked utterly unnerved. At least, until he realized how hard Diana was staring. "The thing is, women shouldn't be allowed to handle money at all," he rushed on, his expression returning to his usual, jackanapes self. Though Diana did note a hint of desperation and beads of sweat forming on his forehead.

"Is that so?" she asked through a clenched jaw.

John assumed a posture of arrogance. "Of course, it is. Everyone knows that women are incapable of handling their own finances. Every woman needs a man to take care of her, to guide and direct her, especially in matters of money. She cannot be expected to sully her delicate mind with coarse matters of commerce and cutthroat financial transactions."

Diana laughed, thinking of her bank balance. "You think I cannot manage my own investments?"

"Of course not," John scoffed. "Why, you're having trouble managing a simple tableau." He gestured to the far end of the stage, where three ladies were now helping Millicent adjust her enormous collar and straighten her wig. "The crowd is growing restless."

Diana narrowed her eyes at him. John knew nothing about growing restless. "Do you think you could do a better job?" she asked, seething.

"Absolutely." His expression brightened to the sort of smile he wore right before he landed them all in mountains of trouble. And he landed them all in trouble often. "In fact, I have a brilliant idea. I will join your Greek tableau."

"What? Don't be preposterous," Diana said. "It's a tableau about strong *women*."

"And what is a strong woman without a man who made her that way?" John asked, stepping to the back of the scene, by the blocks where she and ladies in other scenes would stand. Each block was covered in plain white sheets.

"Good heavens, John, what are you doing?" she hissed as John unbuttoned and removed his coat.

"I'm getting into costume," he said, laughing. "I'm going to be your gallant Spartan warrior."

"I am Athena," Diana argued as he tossed his jacket aside and went to work on the buttons of his waistcoat. "The Athenians and the Spartans were constantly at war."

"As are we, my love, as are we," John said, discarding his waistcoat. He whipped off his necktie, shrugged out of his suspenders, and tugged his shirt out of his trousers next.

"John! Dear God, what are you doing? Stop!" Diana rushed toward him, though she had no idea what she could do to stop his madness.

"I always knew you'd shout my name and call out for God one day," he laughed, dodging out of her reach as she approached him. He pulled the cufflinks out of his sleeves, then peeled his shirt off over his head.

Diana gasped, partially because he was a mad fool to be undressing with half of London on the other side of a thin curtain and half because the sight of his bare chest was exquisite. She'd seen him before on summer holidays at Reese's country house and other places where there'd been swimming, but never at such close proximity. His muscles were strong and well-defined. His broad chest was covered with a pleasingly masculine amount of hair. His trousers hung far too low on his hips, teasing at what might lie under them. Diana was transfixed, even as panic welled up within her.

"Put your clothes back on this instant," she growled, uncertain whether she wanted to chase after him or run away in frustration.

"Come over here and make me," John goaded her. "Or help me arrange this sheet as a toga."

"You are impossible." She marched toward him, reaching for the sheet.

"And you love it," he countered, dodging out of her way as she neared him. "You love me."

"I do not, you lout," she said, even as her heart pounded against her ribs. "I hate you."

"I think you mistake that emotion for another," he laughed, jumping out of her way again. "Shall I remove my trousers as well for authenticity?"

"Don't you dare!"

She chased him back and forth across the tiny area of her scene, grasping for the sheet that he seemed more intent on using to tease her than to wrap around his naked torso. The more Diana leapt after him, the hotter she got. She was certain her whole body was flushed pink with exertion. Indeed, John looked her up and down as though he appreciated the effect.

At last, she grabbed hold of the edge of the sheet and

tugged it toward her, grunting, "You are a right bastard, John Darrow."

All at once, instead of running from her, John slammed up against her, catching her in his arms. "And you love me that way," he said in a breathless, husky voice.

He slanted his mouth over hers, kissing her forcefully. Diana made a sound deep in her throat, but it wasn't a sound of protest. She sagged against him, opening her mouth to him and letting him plunder her mercilessly. His kiss was so devilish and intoxicating that she feared she would lose her mind. She must have lost her mind already to allow him such a salacious liberty. Her friends were likely at the other side of the stage, watching the whole thing.

That thought shocked her back to reality. She tried to pull away from John, catching the briefest glimpse of Bianca holding the others back at the far end of the stage. Bianca wore a look of mischief, as though she actually approved of John's scandalous undertaking.

Diana rebelled at the thought and attempted to jerk away from John. "Unhand me," she panted.

"Never," John growled, leaning in for another kiss.

Diana fought against him, feeling inches away from losing the battle and staying in his arms forever. She refused to give in that easily, though. She wrenched and tugged, twisting in his arms. John laughed as he circled his arms more tightly around her. Diana growled and attempted to wriggle away to one side. She almost made it, but she lost her balance at the last minute. The loss of balance was made worse by the fact that John didn't quite have as tight a hold of her as he could have.

Diana shrieked and grabbed the curtain beside her. But the stage wasn't of sound construction, and instead of holding her upright, the entire curtain tore off its fastenings and dropped. She and John spilled into a tangle of arms and limbs on top of it, John's body covering hers.

The drone of restless conversations from the audience stopped abruptly. It was replaced by a silence so sharp Diana thought she might bleed to death from the way it cut her. Gasps filled the air, along with a few nervous titters. There she was, Lady Diana Pickwick, respected leader of the May Flowers and champion of the rights of women, on her back, legs splayed gracelessly, her Greek costume skewed and showing far more than it should, with bloody John Darrow sprawled on top of her, naked from the waist up.

"Please," she whispered, squeezing her eyes shut. "Please just let me die now."

"I'm so sorry," John whispered back, his voice more serious than Diana had ever heard it.

"What is the meaning of this?" the voice of an elderly woman demanded somewhere nearby. "Is that Lord Whitlock molesting Lady Diana?"

"She doesn't look as though she's being molested to me," a ribald gentleman chuckled.

Diana whimpered at the humiliation, on the edge of tears.

"This is not what it looks like," John said, pushing himself to a kneeling position. Unfortunately, that only proved he was kneeling between Diana's parted legs. He grabbed for the sheet, using it to cover Diana as best he could.

"It looks like something," a woman muttered. Diana prayed for death even more when she saw that woman was Lady Katya Campbell.

"It's all right, everyone, it's all right," Diana's mother said, her voice high-pitched and thin as she and Diana's father pushed their way through the crowd.

Diana groaned, attempting to comport herself and scramble away from John. That was made impossible by the fact that John knelt on the sheet covering her and her costume under it. As soon as he saw the predicament, he helped her recover as best she could. As soon as she was able, they stood. John draped the sheet around her shoulders as modestly as he could, but it was far, far too late.

"It's all right," Diana's mother continued to insist as she swept up to Diana and put an arm around her shoulder. "As Lord Whitlock said, this isn't what it seems."

Diana's father sent John a scathing look that had Diana believing the man's testicles were in serious danger of forcible removal at any time.

"I suppose we should have made the announcement ages ago," Diana's mother went on, laughing nervously. Her face was splotched with red and her eyes were overly bright. "My daughter and Lord Whitlock are engaged, you see."

"What?" Diana and John snapped at the same time.

It was the worst possible thing they could have done, under the circumstances. John seemed to catch that fact and correct himself first. "That is to say, yes, it's true." He laughed tightly and pushed a hand through his hair. "Lady Diana and I are engaged. So this isn't as bad as it looks. No one here has been ruined or had their honor besmirched."

"Not if I have anything to do about it," Diana's father growled, staring daggers at John.

"Yes," Lady Katya spoke up brightly. "I've known about the engagement for a fortnight at least." She pivoted to face the rest of the astounded crowd. "So no one's reputation has been damaged here. The two love-birds were simply anticipating their vows a bit." She laughed as well, pretending everything was right as rain.

A few people nearby laughed uncertainly, then more. Soon, the entire hall was bursting with laughter, as if the whole thing had been another facet of the day's entertainment. Though there was a distinct uneasiness in the air.

"The wedding is in only a few days' time, if you must know," Diana's mother went on, as though making an announcement. "Though it will be a small, private affair." She turned to Diana and John, who had been maneuvered to stand next to each other, glaring at them both.

Diana blinked. "You intend for me to marry this arrogant lout in just a few days' time?" she asked, hoping only her parents and John could hear.

"What else do you propose?" her father asked in clipped tones. "That a daughter of mine be labeled as notorious?"

"Do you have any idea what would happen to your place in society if you do not marry Lord Whitlock?" her mother asked with just as much anger. "You will have no place. You'll have to move to the continent, or worse."

Diana swallowed hard. She felt as though the walls were closing in on her. Damn John and his foolishness. He could have simply proposed to her. But no, he had to go and make a spectacle of her, compromise her in the worst way. Her standing in society was likely already ruined, no matter how much her parents worked to make things right. It was all over for her—her position as leader of the May Flowers, her work for women's rights, her entire life. And on top of that, she would have to marry a man she detested, now more than ever.

"I think I've endured enough humiliation for one day," she said in a low, hoarse voice. "Please excuse me."

As she turned to flee to the farthest, darkest corner she could find, John called after her, "Diana, wait!"

"You will stay right where you are, young man," Diana's father boomed. "You and I need to have a conversation."

Tears flooded Diana's eyes as she scrambled behind the scenery, desperate to dress and hide herself from the world forever. She would never forgive John for destroying her life. Never.

CHAPTER 3

*J*ohn was amazed by how much his life could change in the course of just three days.

"I always intended to marry Diana, but this isn't the way it was supposed to happen," he sighed as he stared at his reflection in the full-length mirror resting in a corner of the chapel's side room.

Harrison chuckled and stepped up to adjust John's necktie. "The whole thing was bound to happen sooner or later. Perhaps you should just consider this as fate giving you a push."

"I'd rather it didn't push me right off a cliff," John grumbled, letting his friend fix his tie and brush the shoulders of his newly-purchased wedding suit.

"If fate hadn't pushed you off a cliff, I'm sure one of us would have done it sooner or later," Freddy said from where he rested against the room's plain bureau. He, too, grinned and seemed amused by the whole mess.

The only one of his friends who wasn't smiling and chuckling and treating the whole thing as a lark was Reese. "I still cannot believe you were such a bloody idiot." Reese nudged Harrison aside and took his place, pinning a boutonniere to John's lapel. He looked as though he wanted to stab John through with the pin. "What madness possessed you to remove your shirt in a public building, knowing there was an audience just a curtain away?"

"I wasn't thinking about that," John confessed in a mumble.

"You weren't thinking about anything," Reese went on, sharp steel in his voice. "You certainly weren't thinking about Diana's reputation. It's utterly ruined now, of course, in spite of this wedding."

Abject misery filled John's gut. "It won't be that bad. This isn't our grandparents' time, after all. Views and morals are so much more liberal today than they were a few generations ago."

"Not this liberal," Reese said, meeting John's eyes and withering him with a look. "I hear that Diana has already had to step down as head of the May Flowers. And Henrietta said she was asked not to speak at an event they're planning next month after all."

"And you know how Diana loves to speak in public," Freddy added, losing some of his humor.

John let out a heavy sigh, rubbing his hands over his

face when Reese stepped aside. "I didn't anticipate any of this. I was only thinking about tweaking her nose and breaking her composure."

"You certainly did that," Harrison said, still grinning.

"I didn't know the curtain would come down," John went on.

"Well, it's come down now," Reese continued his scolding. "In every way possible for Diana. Either you are going to have to make things up to her by being the best and most gracious husband a woman has ever had, or she is going to make your life a living hell."

"Probably both," Freddy said, his lips twitching into a smile.

"As I said," John repeated, "I had always intended to marry her eventually. But only once my financial situation was under control."

"Will it ever be under control, do you think?" Harrison asked, eyes still glittering with mirth.

"It will be, now that he's secured Diana's dowry," Freddy answered for John.

"And I wouldn't count out Diana's own money," Reese added with a thoughtful look. "Not after the way she spoke that afternoon, before disaster struck."

"Diana doesn't have any money." John dismissed the idea without thinking much about it. "I don't either, which is the crux of the problem here." He sighed. "I suppose at some point I'll have to speak to Lord Pickwick and explain the situation."

"You mean you haven't already?" Freddy asked.

"No," John answered sheepishly. "I haven't exactly had heaps of time in the last few days."

Truer words had never been spoken. In the whirlwind seventy-two hours since the emergency engagement, John had been run ragged during every spare minute. He'd sorted practical arrangements with Diana's father, informed his mother of the turn of events, been dragged into the search for an accommodating chapel and minister who could marry them on short notice, and been fitted for wedding clothes. He'd also been forced to search for reasonable accommodations for his mother, who had insisted she couldn't live under the same roof as John and his new bride, now that she would be the dowager viscountess. He'd spent the entire day yesterday touring flats and townhouses in the fashionable neighborhood where several of his mother's friends resided, suspicious about how swiftly his mother had been able to locate suitable places. Almost as if she'd been itching to move away from him and closer to her cronies all along. And he, of course, would pay for the new quarters. With money he didn't have.

"At least we'll be married," he sighed, checking himself in the mirror again. "Perhaps I'll be able to make up for my many faults and the wrongs I've done Diana by bedding her properly."

Harrison and Freddy laughed out loud. "You think you're going to be able to get within ten feet of that woman in a horizontal manner?" Freddy asked.

"After you were already considerably closer than that in the most embarrassing way possible?" Harrison added.

John sent them a miserable look. He wouldn't blame Diana one bit if she refused to let him into her bed. And if he were honest with himself, he probably deserved it.

A knock sounded on the door, releasing John from the conversation and making him wary of what someone else might want from him now. A second later, Danny Long stuck his head around the door.

"Oy, mate. There's a man here to speak to you. Gordon Pratt," Danny said, pushing the door all the way open.

John swallowed hard, his heart sinking to his feet and taking his balls with it. "Mr. Pratt," he croaked, rushing to the doorway. "What brings you here this afternoon?"

"I've got a proposition for you," Pratt said in his usual, cheerful voice. The man was rail thin with a gap between his front teeth. He spoke like a gentleman, but John knew for a fact he was the son of a greengrocer. Well, a greengrocer who had opened five separate shops under the same name and made enough money to mingle with high society and send his son to Oxford.

"Now is not a good time, Pratt," John said in a low voice, glancing over his shoulder at his friends.

"Oh, I think you'd better talk to the man," Danny laughed. Of course, Danny probably knew all about who Pratt was and what his business ventures were. Danny was a man of commerce as well, even though he'd befriended their group of aristocrats and married Lady Phoebe Darlington.

John send Danny a troubled look, hoping he'd keep quiet, then stepped into the hall with Pratt.

"He's the bloke who lost all of John's money," Danny told the others as soon as John was in the hall, proving that the man had no discretion whatsoever.

"Today is not a good day, Pratt," John said, grabbing Pratt by the arm and walking him farther down the hall. They stopped beside a door that was cracked open.

"I would think that today is the very best of days for you, my lord," Pratt said in a jovial tone. "Felicitations on your marriage, by the by."

"Thank you," John said distractedly. "But if that's all you came to say, you could have waited."

"Time and money wait for no man, my lord," Pratt said, the avaricious gleam in his eyes making John squirm. "Especially not when you're about to have a beautiful new wife who might just have the blunt to cover the tens of thousands of pounds you owe me."

A thump sounded nearby, as though someone had knocked something over. It had John's nerves frazzled, so he moved Pratt farther down the hall toward the exit.

"I cannot use my bride's money to pay my debts," he said in clipped tones, sweat pouring down his back. "It wouldn't be right."

"Well, you're going to have to use someone's money," Pratt said. "I've extended your payment window as much as I can."

"I've been sending you regular payments," John told him with more than a hint of pleading. "That's the best I can do."

"I'll tell you what." Pratt shifted his weight, smiling in a way that sent a chill down John's spine. "I've got another investment opportunity on the horizon. There's a bloke who has a brilliant idea for a combustion engine. Says it's a new design and that it could make investors a fortune."

"No." John shook his head emphatically. "No more investing. I was wrong to give you any money in the first place."

"Suit yourself, then." Pratt shrugged. "But you still owe me thirty thousand, give or take a pound or two. I need it soon. I'm a nice man, my lord, but only so nice."

"You'll have your money," John promised. "One way or another." Though God only knew how. He was in so far over his head that he didn't think he'd see the light of day ever again.

DIANA'S HEART NEARLY POPPED OUT OF HER THROAT when she knocked over the candlestick sitting on the bureau where her wedding jewelry and flowers sat. She'd thought for certain John would realize she could hear his conversation when he and the man with him moved away from the door of the dressing room where she and Bea were preparing for the wedding.

"He owes that much money?" Bea whispered, her eyes round and alarmed.

Diana was alarmed as well, but underneath the initial shock of overhearing how much money John owed, her heart throbbed with excitement. She had John on the back foot in the most astounding way possible.

She touched her finger to her lips to signal Bea into silence, then crept closer to the door to continue to listen.

"You still owe me thirty thousand, give or take a pound or two," the man with John said.

Diana's jaw dropped. The sum was so staggering that she didn't truly hear the final exchange of the conversation. John promised to get the man his money, then walked back down the hall to the room she assumed he'd been given to prepare for the ceremony. The man to whom he owed the money started to leave, chuckling to himself.

Diana leapt into action, pulling open the door and thrusting her head out into the hall. She waited until John had ducked back into his dressing room before chasing after John's friend.

"Excuse me," she called out, catching him in the hall leading to the main part of the chapel. "What is your name, sir?"

The man turned toward her, his eyes popping wide, his gap-toothed grin appreciative. "Gordon Pratt, at your service, my lady." He raked her up and down, taking in the sight of her in her wedding dress. "I daresay Lord Whitlock is a lucky man."

"Lord Whitlock is a rank bastard and a prick," she growled, rushing to stand as close to Mr. Pratt as she dared. She glanced up and down the hall to make certain no one was listening in, then asked, "By any chance do you have a card for your place of business?" As a quick after though, she added, "I assume you are some sort of an investment broker?"

"That I am, my lady. Were you interested in expanding your pin money a bit?" He reached into the inner pocket of his jacket and took out a card.

As soon as he handed it over, Diana made a sound of triumph. Along with Mr. Pratt's name, the address of his office was listed on the card. That was all she needed at the moment. "Mr. Pratt, might I pay you a call tomorrow?"

Mr. Pratt blinked. "Tomorrow, my lady? Won't you be celebrating your nuptials, if you know what I mean." He winked lasciviously at her.

"Certainly not." Diana snapped straight, then turned and marched back to the other hallway and her dressing room. Let the impertinent man make what he would of her abrupt departure. She would deal with him tomorrow. For the moment, it was of vital importance that no one, least of all John, saw her speaking to him or noticed that she'd taken his card.

"What are you doing, Diana?" Bea asked, nearly beside herself with alarm when Diana slipped back into the dressing room.

"If John thinks that this is going to be a marriage like

any other marriage, he has another think coming," Diana said with a triumphant smile. She crossed to the corner of the room where the dress and shoes she'd arrived at the chapel wearing were stored, and tucked Mr. Pratt's card into the small purse she always carried with her. "He thinks that a woman needs a man to handle her financial arrangements? Well, let's see how he feels when the tables are turned."

"You aren't planning to school your husband about finance, are you?" Bea looked at her strangely.

"I would never do anything as simple and straightforward as that," Diana said with a laugh. "No, I plan to teach John a lesson in another way."

"What other way?" Bea asked.

Diana chewed her lip and paced a circle around the room. "I'm not certain yet, but I know I'll come up with something."

Her pacing and her thoughts were interrupted a minute later as her mother swept into the room.

"Oh, my poor, dear girl," she said, as weepy as she'd been since the horrific incident at the hall. "You must be beside yourself. Believe me, if I could have invented any other way to make this damnable situation right, I would have erased the whole thing from everyone's memory."

Diana sighed at her mother's theatrics and let the woman embrace her. "Truly, Mama, it's not as bad as all that."

"It is, my dear, it is," her mother wept. "Your reputation is ruined, your honor has been brought into question, and you are now being forced to marry a man that I know you detest."

Several conflicting emotions struck Diana at once. The initial sting of having her social life decimated had abated—though she was certain it would be renewed again and again, every time she was denied entrance or invitation to an event she had her heart set on—and now she was mostly concerned with ways she could seek out her revenge on her groom. The fun of turning the thumb screws on John would just about make up for her humiliation. But she did carry a hefty amount of remorse for her mother's distress.

It went against everything Diana believed, but as she patted her mother's back, she said, "Mama, if you must know, I don't hate John nearly as much as I've let on over the years."

"Of course, you do, darling." Her mother sniffed, straightening. She dabbed at her eyes with her handkerchief as she said, "You've despised the man for years, and with good reason. He's vexed you at every turn and driven away several far more docile suitors."

Diana let out a breath. "Mama, I've hated John all this time for not proposing sooner."

Her mother blinked. "I beg your pardon?"

"I've wanted to marry the bastard for ages," Diana confessed.

"Diana! That language is not becoming for a lady of your station," her mother scolded.

"Perhaps not, but the sentiment is true," Diana said.

"So please don't think that you've consigned me to a life of misery by pretending this marriage was arranged ages ago. I am very much looking forward to being Lady Whitlock, just as I'm looking forward to making my husband's every waking moment utter torture."

Her mother stared at her. "You've wanted to marry the man for ages...and you wish to torment him once you do?"

"Precisely." Diana smiled.

"We are ready to begin," her father said, stepping into the open doorway.

"Do you hear that, Mama?" Diana said, glancing to Bea—who handed her the wedding bouquet—then marching for the door. "We're ready to begin. And what a beginning it's going to be."

She walked right past her father in the doorway and strode ahead to the chapel by herself. There were few guests in attendance, considering the circumstances of the marriage, which was fine as far as Diana was concerned. John had already taken up his position at the front of the chapel with Harrison by his side. Freddy and Reese were there with him, as were Fergus and Henrietta O'Shea, Rupert and Cecelia Campbell, Bianca and Jack, Natalia and Linus, and even Lady Katya and Lord Malcolm Campbell. Danny Long rushed in from the side corridor with his wife, Lady Phoebe, at the last moment as Diana marched up the center aisle, a look of determination plastered on her face.

"You look astounding," John told her in a breathless voice, his face a mask of happiness, in spite of the situation they found themselves in. "Truly the most beautiful thing I've ever seen."

Diana smiled genuinely in spite of herself. John was delightful to look at himself in his smart suit with his hair combed rakishly. She truly could have done worse in a husband. But most delightful of all, John clearly didn't know what sort of trouble was about to rain down on him.

He offered his arm, and Diana took it. "I'm glad to see you smiling," he whispered as the minister began the opening part of the marriage ceremony. "It's a bit of a relief, if I'm being honest."

"A relief?" Diana asked, blinking innocently at him.

"Yes." John lowered his voice even more. "I was certain you'd be furious with me over this whole thing, all things considered. I thought you might back out at the last moment."

"Now why would I do a thing like that?" Diana asked, her smile broader than ever. Bless him for being a clueless fool.

He smiled as if reassured. "I promise I'll make you happy, Diana," he vowed. "Regardless of the circumstances around us."

She was touched by his earnestness, whether she wanted to be or not. She'd known John long enough to reluctantly admit that, underneath his impishness and frivolity, he was a good man. Chances were that they would end up happy together in the end. But first, she had revenge to enact.

"I promise I will give you everything you deserve," she said, smiling at him with false sweetness.

John had the good sense to lose his smile and look very nervous indeed.

CHAPTER 4

*D*iana supposed that the full wedding service would have flown by like a dream if one were truly delighted to be marrying one's groom. It wasn't that she didn't want to marry John. She was close to being able to admit to herself that she'd wanted to marry him for years. But anticipation of what came next and thoughts about what she could do with the information she'd learned about John's financial status rattled through her head, making her impatient for the whole thing to be over.

"And do you, Diana Elizabeth Pickwick, take this man, John Theodore Sullivan Darrow, to be your lawfully wedded husband, to love, honor, and obey 'til death do you part?" the minister asked, snapping Diana out of her thoughts. She's been so caught up in those thoughts that she'd barely listened to a word of the ceremony and had hardly registered John saying he would love, honor, and cherish her.

Diana hesitated. She met John's eyes and held them. The man was practically squirming and looked as though he desperately wanted to adjust the collar of his stiff, new suit. Diana let a slow, clever grin spread across her face and narrowed her eyes, knowing full well the effect her expression produced. Sure enough, John swallowed anxiously.

"I'm not certain about the 'obey' part," she muttered, hoping that only John could hear, "but I do." Her grin widened fully and she flickered one eyebrow at John before turning to the minister with an innocent smile worthy of the most overjoyed bride.

"Then, by the power invested in me by God and by His holy church, I now pronounce you husband and wife," the minister said with a relieved smile before continuing on to conclude the ceremony.

That was it. After years of antagonism and vexation, Diana was married to John at last. When they turned to greet their families as husband and wife, the looks they were met with were as relieved as the minister's had been. Relief with a touch of anxiety, as though no one was completely certain the hasty marriage would do the trick. Diana rather thought it wouldn't. She had the horrible feeling that, thanks to John's antics, she would forever be a pariah.

But at least she now had him right where she wanted

him, and she intended to take full advantage of whatever power remained to her.

"I think the wedding was beautiful, when all is said and done," Bea told Diana in her usual cheery voice once they had all retired to Whitlock House for a modest tea. The simple offering was meant to take the place of the sort of grand reception that Diana's marriage would have had, were it not an event more suited to the gossip pages than those filled with happy announcements.

"I dare say Diana is one of the finest beauties in London, no matter what circumstances her beauty shines in," Reese commented graciously. He had joined the circle of ladies huddled protectively around Diana rather than joining the scrum of men with John at the opposite end of the parlor.

"Our Diana will always be considered one of England's finest beauties," Cecelia Campbell added, just as gracious as Reese. But then, Cece always had been the most refined and forgiving one of their circle of friends. Once she had forgiven her husband, Rupert, for running off to join the army, delaying their marriage for four years, that was. "And I predict that, once the dust has settled, you and John will be perfectly happy together, as Rupert and I are, in spite of the sins of the past."

Diana did her best to return Cece's optimistic comment with a smile, but her heart was still thumping with frustration and her mind spinning as it sought out ideas to get back at John rather than settle with him.

"And you are beyond fortunate to get to live in such a

gorgeous home," Bea said, glancing around at Whitlock House's massive parlor. She sighed happily as her eyes landed on a life-sized portrait of John's ancestor, Lord Sullivan Whitlock, and his family. "They look as though they made quite a happy life in this house, and I'm certain you will as well."

Diana could only hum and arch one eyebrow at the comment. "I will as soon as I can determine how best to impress upon my dear husband just what I think of him and this whole mess."

Her friends displayed a full spectrum of reactions to her words. Bianca laughed out loud and looked proud of Diana for her moxie. Cece looked mildly shocked, her pretty face coloring. Reese's smile dropped to an anxious frown.

"Perhaps I should warn John to be on his guard," he said, taking a half step back from the ladies and turning toward the cluster of gentlemen.

"You can warn him all you'd like," Diana said, "but no matter how he prepares, he won't be ready for what is about to rain down on him."

Again, Bianca laughed, then covered her mouth with one hand. Natalia reacted similarly, while Bea and Cece shook their heads.

"I'll tell him that," Reese said, relaxing back into an amused smile before walking away to join the men.

Diana watched as he joined the other group. Reese leaned in to deliver her message to John immediately. John's stoic expression gave way to a look of shock and terror, and when he snapped up and glanced across the room to Diana, she fueled that terror by giving him a cat-like grin. The color seemed to drain from John's face as he turned back to his friends, probably seeking advice.

"Oh, how I wish I could be a fly on the wall for whatever interactions you and your dear groom have next," Bianca said with a wistful sigh.

"I wouldn't wish that for anything," Bea said, her eyes widening. "What comes next is their wedding night, after all."

Diana would have found it charming that Bea's face turned bright red and she glanced down with a mysterious smile, but the wedding night was just another hurdle she would have to get over in her emergency marriage. It was, however, a hurdle she could use.

"Now that Reese has joined the others, it's time we ladies school you on a few things you will need to know for your wedding night," Bianca said, turning her back to the men and forming something of a wall with Natalia to hide their conversation from any prying ears.

Diana made an ironic sound and shook her head. "There's no need to educate me on what goes on in the marriage bed," she said, raising one hand.

Cece blinked in surprise. "Don't tell me that you and John have already...." She let her sentence drop with a significant look.

"Heavens, no," Diana laughed. Though her heart twisted to admit as much. Not that it would have been proper for anything else to have happened between her and John. She would be lying to herself if she said she hadn't thought about it and dreamed about it and longed for it. She shook her head and went on with, "All of my friends are married women. And you must admit, the lot of you are woefully indiscreet when it comes to discussing private matters."

"We are not," Bea defended herself, growing even redder in the face.

"Perhaps not you, dear." Diana took her hand and patted it. She glanced on to Natalia and Bianca. "Others are not so close-lipped about things."

"I don't believe in keeping young women ignorant of sexuality," Bianca said, tilting her chin up. "It denigrates women and puts them at a dangerous disadvantage when they travel out into the world. Why, if you only knew the number of women in Clerkenwell who have found themselves in delicate situations because they were led into dalliances by men who took advantage of their ignorance, you would feel the same way."

"Your charity work is admirable, Bianca," Diana said, her mouth twitching into a grin. "And I am certain you do everything you can to help those unfortunate young women recover from the great wrongs that are done to them. But I didn't need to know about that trick you discovered to prevent yourself from gagging while enjoying your husband." She crossed her arms and sent Bianca a challenging look for good measure.

"You might not have needed it *at the time*," Bianca said, emphasizing the last words, as though Diana would be able to use the knowledge soon, "but others found it quite edifying."

"Yes, they did," Cece said quietly, her cheeks going bright pink.

Diana let out a huff and uncrossed her arms. "Do you see? This is why I have no need of any special conversations, though my mother did try last night."

"Good Lord," Bianca said, looking horrified. "Mothers should never attempt such things."

"Our mother did an admirable job," Natalia said with a shrug.

"Your mother had no need to instruct Bianca, considering the entire purpose of her marriage was because Jack had already conceived his heir," Cece added, her saucy grin still in place.

Bianca cleared her throat. "Yes, well, let's not revisit old scandals. We're here for Diana's benefit now."

"And I can assure you, my dear friends," Diana said, "that I have no need of your help or advice. For one, I have no intention whatsoever of allowing John any of his so-called marital rights. At least, not anytime soon." She crossed her arms again and stared menacingly across the parlor at John.

John chose just that moment to glance over at her. The expression that hit him was everything Diana could have hoped for and more. Her dear husband was intimidated down to his core.

"I doubt that will last long," Bianca said with a laugh. "You two have been circling each other like exotic birds in a mating dance for years. I wager you won't last out the week before you're panting his name in ecstasy."

Diana pulled her gaze away from John to raise her eyebrows at her friend. "If you think that, you are unaware of a few extenuating circumstances."

"Extenuating circumstances?" Natalia asked, looking thrilled by the prospect.

Diana leaned in, causing her friends to do the same. "I've just found out that John has racked up a great deal of debt," she whispered. Gratifyingly, her friends all looked shocked. That meant that, for a change, she wasn't the last to know a vital piece of information. "He owes shocking sums of money to some sort of investor or broker. For all I know, the man could be from the underworld."

"Hell?" Bea asked, looking shocked.

"No, darling," Diana told her. "The world of criminals."

"John has his faults, but I doubt he'd become involved with criminals," Bianca said. "Not when one of his closest friends is an assistant commissioner of Scotland Yard." Bianca's husband, Jack, had held that position since Bianca's father had arranged for the job in order to make Jack worthy of Bianca's hand.

"You make a good point." Diana tilted her head to one side, the gears in her brain turning even faster. "But that also gives me ideas."

"Lord save us from your ideas," Bianca said, looking as though she would very much like to be part of them.

"But isn't John being so badly in debt a bad thing?" Bea asked, biting her lip. "Won't that add salt to the wound of what he's done to ruin your social standing?"

"Not when I have the resources to pay his debts," Diana said with a triumphant grin.

Natalia snorted with laughter and clapped a hand over her mouth. Cece looked impressed.

Bianca did not. "How is bailing John out anything other than rewarding the louse for trapping you in this marriage?"

Diana furrowed her brow, staring across the room at John once more. "I'm not certain yet, but as soon as I am, I'll let you know."

The reception continued as jovially as any reception for a wedding caused by a ruinous scandal could. At least the group that had gathered for the celebrations was close enough that most of their friends stayed through the afternoon, then joined Diana and John for supper. All in all, it made for a lively party, though any outsider would be hard pressed to distinguish it as a wedding supper rather than just another loud gathering of a particularly closely-knit circle of friends.

It wasn't until Diana and John said goodbye to their guests well after dark and headed upstairs that things grew tense.

"I've, er, had the guest room across the hall from the viscount's suite prepared, just in case," John said as they mounted the stairs and turned down the hall that led to the cluster of rooms reserved for the private use of the lord and lady of the house.

Diana blinked innocently at him. "And why would you do that?" she asked. Her plot for the night involved him sharing a bed with her. The torture would be so much more acute that way.

A glimmer of hope shone in John's eyes, and his usual, impish grin looked as though it might return. "I just thought," he began, "under the circumstances and all, seeing as things unraveled so quickly...."

"Things?" She stopped and turned to face him as they reached the door to the master bedroom suite. John's mother had given her a quick tour of her new home the day before, as every servant in the house busied themselves moving her things, John's things, and John's mother's things to various new rooms appropriate to the change in station.

John stared back at her and cleared his throat. "Considering how we ended up in this mess," he said in a softer tone that was likely designed to be intimate.

Diana wasn't ready to let him get comfortable yet. "Oh." She put as little meaning into the single syllable as she could. Let John twist himself into knots trying to figure out what she meant.

The master suite consisted of a large bedroom furnished in a delightfully modern style. It also contained a fully modernized bathroom, complete with running water. Diana was pleasantly surprised to discover that John had had those sorts of renovations done. Every fashionable house in London was caught up in the craze of having their houses plumbed. If Diana were still in a position to be admitted into society drawing rooms and the like, it would have been something she could brag about. Doors on the other side of the room led to two separate dressing rooms, one for the viscount and one for the viscountess. Diana's things had already been moved into the more feminine dressing room, so she swept across the room and entered, closing that door behind her, without sparing a look for John.

As soon as she was alone, she let out a quick laugh. John was already on the back foot, and if she had her way, he would be even more so before the night was done. She'd specifically told the upstairs maid who was in training to be her lady's maid that she wouldn't need help that night, which meant she was left to remove her wedding gown herself. The maid—and everyone else in the house—had probably assumed John would be doing the honors. They could believe what they wanted to.

After struggling with the fastenings and finally ripping the poor dress when she couldn't adequately reach all of the buttons, Diana tossed the elaborate garment aside and slithered into a plain and rather dowdy nightgown. That would be the first punishment John would receive, for she had it on good authority from her friends that the only thing more tempting to a man than a lacy and elegant nightgown was one that covered everything, leaving the man to wonder and hope.

Indeed, as soon as she stepped back into the

bedroom, John's eyes filled with an expectant kind of fire. He was already in bed, seated with his back against a stack of pillows. He wore pajamas of his own, but Diana was quick to note that the top few buttons of his shirt were undone, revealing a tantalizing peek at the attractive chest she'd seen all of the other day. He sat straighter as she reached the bed and pulled back the covers to slip inside.

"You look...lovely," he said, raking her with a glance.

"Thank you," Diana replied without looking at him.

She settled into her side of the bed, pretending with everything she had that she was disinterested. In fact, her heart raced and she could feel a flush spreading over her skin. *All* of her skin. Her breasts felt heavy, and her nipples were more sensitive than usual to the brush of fabric against them as she found a comfortable position. Her sex ached—a feeling that was not helped at all by the knowledge that, if she wanted it, she could have John between her legs within seconds.

"Well, goodnight, then," she told John lying on her back and pulling the covers up to her chin.

John hesitated before asking, "Goodnight?"

Diana sent him a look as though she were baffled by what he could mean saying the word like that. "It is night-time, is it not?" She blinked innocently at him.

"Nighttime on our wedding night," he said, squirming a bit. The movement brought him closer to her.

Under the covers, Diana could feel the heat of his

body, so close to pressing against hers. She had to fight with a primal part of herself that wanted everything she was entitled to as a married woman. "How very clever of you to remember what day it is," she said, dripping with sarcasm.

John cleared his throat and flinched back a bit. "All right. I suppose I deserve this punishment."

"You do," she told him, breaking her icy character for a moment. "You most certainly do."

"It would be good for both of us, you know," he said, attempting a sultry tone. "That is to say, there are other ways I could make things up to you." He reached for her under the covers, slipping his hand across her belly.

It was all Diana could do to remain stiff and feign disinterest. His lightest touch had her blood heating within her and her body throbbing for more. But that would be conceding defeat in a way her pride couldn't take. She was determined to make John work for what, admittedly, they both wanted.

"No," she said. She met his eyes with as steely a look as she could manage. "I'm saying no." She paused. "Are you going to charge mindlessly ahead and force this too, the way you forced this entire marriage?"

John jerked fully away from her. Diana fought not to wince. She wished she'd planned out what she was going to say in advance, because what came out was decidedly too harsh.

"Perhaps a kiss goodnight," she said with a sigh,

scrambling for a way to keep his leash taut without hurting him outright.

John softened. "I will accept a kiss," he said, "knowing that a kiss, and only a kiss, is fitting punishment for my actions." He inched closer to her. "But, Diana, I *am* sorry," he said, genuine contrition in his tone.

Before she could reply, he leaned down to close his mouth over hers. It felt delicious to be kissed while lying on her back. John was an accomplished kisser to begin with. He caressed her lips with his and brushed his tongue against her until she let him in. His tongue teased hers with just enough insistence to leave her body humming, but not enough to make her feel as though she were in any danger. At least, not that kind of danger. One sensual kiss, and she feared she was in serious danger of abandoning her plan to remain frosty altogether.

She was on the precipice of giving in and letting him have his way with her when he pulled back. The kiss left them both panting. Diana's whole body was alive with heat and longing, and she could feel a warm wetness between her thighs that only made her want John more. It took every bit of strength she had to take a deep breath and say, "Well, goodnight, then."

She twisted to face away from him as quickly as she could, so John wouldn't see the hunger in her eyes.

John cleared his throat and said, "Goodnight, Diana," in a heavy voice.

He got up to turn the lights off, which came as a relief to Diana. Without light, he couldn't see how much she wanted him. She had a giddy feeling that Bianca was right and would win her wager, because after that one kiss, Diana was certain she wouldn't be able to hold out past a week. Which meant she had to execute her revenge as soon as possible.

CHAPTER 5

*D*iana found it nearly impossible to sleep. Between the throbbing in particularly sensitive parts of her body caused by the acute awareness of John sleeping mere inches away from her and the implications of all that meant, all the ways her life had changed, sleep eluded her. The fact wasn't helped at all by her inability to tell whether John was awake as well or if the bastard had drifted off into a peaceful slumber. His breathing was suspiciously steady, but he could have been pretending for her benefit, as she was pretending for his. At least the restless night gave her the advantage of allowing her to come up with a plan to exact her revenge.

By morning, she had the whole thing planned out. She slipped out of bed before John could awaken from the sleep he'd finally fallen into, washed and dressed with lightning speed, then hurried downstairs for breakfast. The dowager Lady Whitlock was already seated at the breakfast table when Diana arrived, which meant she was forced to slow down and muddle through a polite conversation with the woman. Her new mother-in-law seemed intent on wheedling information about the wedding night from Diana, but Diana greeted those questions with smiling silence, hoping the woman would draw her own conclusions.

She was nearly finished with her breakfast and ready to put her plan in motion when John entered the room. He paused briefly in the doorway, sending a questioning look Diana's way before saying, "This is a lovely sight. My two favorite ladies breakfasting together."

"Your bride and I were just having a pleasant talk," John's mother said, sending Diana a fond smile.

Diana felt guilty for disappointing the woman as she stood and said, "Yes, and unfortunately, I have pressing matters I must attend to immediately this morning."

John's smile faded as Diana approached him in the doorway. "Pressing matters?"

"That I must attend to immediately," she repeated herself. The smile she sent him was designed to put him off-balance.

"I was rather hoping we could spend the day together," he said, following Diana into the hall.

Diana winced before turning back to him. Perhaps she did owe John more than a nod and a wave the day after their wedding. If they were going to build any sort of successful future together, they would have to find a way to interact with each other that didn't leave them both wanting to scream. At least, not that way.

"I need to visit my solicitor," she told him simply. "The wedding happened so swiftly that I did not have a chance to put some of my financial matters in order."

"Ah yes, your great and illustrious financial matters," John said with a teasing glint in his eyes. "Because ladies should work for their financial independence, whether they're married or not."

In an instant, her back was up. "Yes, that is exactly what I meant," she snapped. She stepped closer to him, challenging him with a look. "It is clear that you do not think much of women responsibly shepherding their own money."

"Shepherding!" His brow flew up and his face lit with mirth. "I am in favor of it if it means you will wear a darling shepherdess's costume." He leaned closer to her, his expression and tone dropping into lasciviousness as he went on with, "I wouldn't mind that at all."

Diana let out an exasperated breath. Just like that, things were back to the way they had always been between the two of them. She shouldn't have expected anything less. At least it made her plans for the day that much more enjoyable.

"Think of it what you like, but I take financial matters seriously," she said, unable to resist sending him an arch look. The last thing she wanted to do was reveal that she knew all about his financial situation, which meant it was necessary for her to walk away from him at a fast clip.

"Diana, I am sorry," John called after her. "Please, let me make it up to you by...by taking you to Hyde Park this afternoon or to the theater tonight."

"So all of London can point and laugh at the lady whose reputation was ruined?" Diana called back over her shoulder. "I don't think so."

She marched on, snatching her hat and coat from the cabinet where her lady's maid in training had left them on Diana's request. As soon as she had her hat affixed to her hair and her purse in hand, she stomped out the door and into London.

It was easy enough to hail a cab to take her to the address printed on the card Mr. Pratt had given her. The man's office was located in a surprisingly elegant part of the city. Its furnishings were sleek and modern, which impressed Diana. At least John had lost his money to a man who appeared to know what he was doing, in part. She also found it encouraging that she was met in the front part of the office by a clerk who was neat and appeared to be organized.

"Let me just see if Mr. Pratt is seeing clients yet, my lady," the lad said after Diana introduced herself.

He nodded, then disappeared into a side room. Diana heard the indistinct sounds of a conversation, then almost right away, Mr. Pratt stepped out into the main part of the office.

"Lady Whitlock," he said with his large, gap-toothed smile.

It took Diana a few seconds to realize that she was

Lady Whitlock now. She blinked, then put on a smile, facing the man. "Mr. Pratt."

"And what brings a fine lady like yourself to my humble office the day after your auspicious wedding?" Mr. Pratt asked, gesturing for Diana to come with him into his office.

Diana glanced warily to the clerk, then to another man, who was waiting in a corner of the room and looking far too interested in why Diana was there for her comfort. She kept her lips pressed shut and walked with Mr. Pratt into his office. Part of her questioned the propriety of closeting herself alone with the man, but it wasn't as though her reputation could be damaged any further. And if she conducted her business as quickly as possible, no one would ever find out she'd been there.

"Please, have a seat, my lady." Mr. Pratt offered her one of the chairs in front of his desk as he himself walked around it. He waited to be seated.

"I don't think I will, Mr. Pratt," she said.

Her refusal to sit meant he had to stand as well, so he crossed back around his desk to study her with a curious look. "What can I do for you, my lady?" he asked.

"I will be brief, sir," Diana began. "I wish to pay off my husband's debts."

Mr. Pratt's eyes widened. Then he burst into laughter. "What a lovely sentiment, my lady."

He continued to chuckle as she withdrew a small ledger from her bank that contained, among other things, the total amount of money held in her accounts. Once she opened the ledger to the correct page, she showed it to him.

Mr. Pratt immediately stopped laughing. He stood straighter, clearing his throat, and gaped at the balance recorded on the pages in front of him.

"As I said, Mr. Pratt, I wish to pay off my husband's debt," Diana repeated.

Mr. Pratt glanced suspiciously from the ledger to Diana. "How do I know this is real?" he asked. "How does a woman have that much money in her name?"

Irritated but unsurprised, Diana flipped the ledger to the first page and showed it to Mr. Pratt again. "Are you familiar with the executives of the Bank of London, Mr. Pratt? Do you happen to know their names, and are you familiar with their signatures?"

Her ledger was a complete record of every transaction she'd made in the five years since opening her accounts. Various parts of it were signed and notarized by high-ranking officials within the bank. She'd gone to the trouble in case just this sort of thing would happen. Men like Mr. Pratt—and like John—needed verification of what they didn't want to see.

Fortunately, Mr. Pratt seemed to accept the proof in front of him. "Well, I'll be a monkey's uncle," he said, raking a hand through his hair in surprise. He looked at Diana with newfound respect. "You could buy Lord Whitlock's debt ten times over."

"I am aware of that, sir," Diana said.

"I'll make up the documents right away and arrange

for the transfer of funds," he said, moving back behind his desk. "And if you're interested, my lady, I have several investment opportunities that a woman such as yourself would be highly interested in," he added with a smile.

"Considering that you lost over thirty thousand pounds belonging to my husband, I think not," Diana said. Besides which, she already had a reputable investment advisor, and she preferred to choose all of her investments herself.

"Understood, my lady," Mr. Pratt said as he busied himself with papers behind his desk. "But you have my card, just in case."

"I do," Diana said. Her mouth twitched into a grin. "I do" was what she'd said to John less than twenty-four hours before. "One other thing, Mr. Pratt," she went on, feeling a surge of power over the ease of pulling off the first part of her revenge plot. "Under no circumstances whatsoever will you reveal to Lord Whitlock who has redeemed him."

"My lady?" Mr. Pratt glanced up with a confused frown.

"I have another story I would like for you to tell him, sir," Diana went on. "It is a very particular story, one that has been thoroughly thought out, and you must repeat it to him verbatim. Do you understand?"

A mischievous look appeared in Mr. Pratt's eyes, as if he, too, were up for a little fun. "I understand completely, my lady."

"Good," Diana said, grinning like a fiend. "This is what I'd like you to tell my erstwhile husband."

JOHN HAD HOPED THAT THE DAY AFTER HIS WEDDING would provide him with an opportunity to make things right with Diana. He felt like a damn fool for landing them in the mess they were in, and all he wanted was to find a way to restore Diana's reputation, not to mention her faith in him. Not that he'd done much in the last few years to inspire any faith from her at all. In fact, the more he examined his behavior and actions in the last few years, the worse he felt about things. What had seemed like fun and games just a week ago now seemed appalling on his part.

"Don't you worry, my boy," his mother said as she finished her breakfast tea. "You've started this marriage on the wrong foot, yes, but you and Diana have been friends for ages."

"I'm not sure that we have, Mama," John confessed, poking at the yolk of his eggs with his fork. He had no appetite for breakfast at all, which was alarming in the extreme.

"Of course, you have," his mother chuckled, standing and moving to his end of the table. "I've watched the two of you interact for all this time. I know two souls who are friends and who are meant for each other when I see them."

"I've behaved abominably toward her," John sighed. "I've teased and tormented her whenever I could."

"My point exactly," his mother said.

John glanced doubtfully up at her.

"If she were anything other than your dearest friend, she never would have put up with any of it," his mother went on. "She would have given you a tight slap the first time you tried anything childish and you never would have seen her or heard from her again."

"We have the same friends," he argued. "She's been forced to put up with me."

His mother laughed. "And you think she couldn't have gotten out of it? She couldn't have found other friends?"

John tilted his head to the side. Perhaps his mother had a point. As wretched as he'd been, Diana had come back for more, over and over. She'd given as good as she got too. Perhaps there was hope after all.

There had been hope in the kiss they'd shared the night before. John was certain that if he had pressed things even a tiny bit, Diana would have caved to him. They could have made love in spectacular fashion, and perhaps then all would have been forgiven. But he hadn't deserved to make love to the woman he loved. Not yet. Not until he smoothed over the destruction of Diana's social standing. Not until he sorted out his own miserable affairs.

He abandoned his breakfast to take the first steps in making things right. Those first steps just happened to be swallowing his pride and doing something he should have done a long time ago.

"Harrison, I need your help." He went straight to his best friend's house with the intention of borrowing at least enough money to satisfy Pratt temporarily.

"Always," Harrison said, getting up from the desk in his office, where the butler had shown John, and coming around to speak to him as friends. "Whatever you need, it's yours."

"How about five thousand pounds?" John said, instantly wincing. It wasn't even close to the full amount of his debt, but it was a huge amount to borrow from even the closest friend.

Sure enough, Harrison looked stunned for a moment. "Of course, I'll juggle things as best I can to give it to you," he stammered, flushing slightly.

"I know it's a monumental thing to ask," John sighed, breaking into pacing in front of Harrison. "I don't know what else to do, though. Pratt needs to be paid. I could liquidate a few resources to make a dent in the debt, but Mama has her heart set on a flat near to her friends. God only knows what expenses Diana will have. And should we have children...." He blew out a breath, rubbing a hand over his face.

"I understand," Harrison said. "And I'm here to help." He started for the door. "We'll go to your Mr. Pratt's office to see how much he'll take as repayment in good faith, then we'll find a way to get the rest of it."

John felt miserable for asking so much of a friend.

Owing so much money was emasculating in the extreme, but if he ever wanted to regain his pride and his confidence, he would need to start somewhere. Diana deserved the best husband she could possibly have, and since the vows had already been spoken, that husband would have to be him.

They made their way across London to Pratt's office, stopping at Harrison's bank so that his friend could check his balances and know just how much help he could offer. The whole time, John did his best to talk himself into believing that what he was doing was, in fact, brave, and that as soon as he sorted things, he would be able to give Diana the life she deserved.

By the time they reached Pratt's office, announcing themselves to his clerk, John was convinced that redemption was possible.

"Mr. Pratt will see you now," the clerk announced with surprising speed, ushering them into Pratt's office.

"Lord Whitlock, how nice to see you," Pratt greeted him, coming around his desk with a hand extended. John noted a curious glimmer in the man's eyes. Pratt seemed to be having trouble keeping a straight face as well.

"Pratt." John nodded, shaking the man's hand. "You know my friend, Lord Landsbury."

"My lord." Pratt nodded solemnly to Harrison, then turned back to John. "What can I do for you today, my lord?"

"I've come to see if we can negotiate my debt." John dove right into things.

Pratt's face twitched. "Ah. Your debt."

"Yes, my debt." A sudden prickle of anxiety shot down John's back.

"The thing is, my lord," Pratt said, his expression as perplexing as ever, "you no longer owe that debt to me."

John blinked, a feeling of dread filling him. "Are you...are you telling me...have you perhaps...forgiven my debt?"

Pratt laughed. "Would it were that easy, my lord," he said. "In fact, your debt has been purchased."

John swallowed hard. "Purchased?" the single word came out choked.

"I didn't think this was the sort of place to go selling gentlemen's debts," Harrison said in alarm.

"Under usual circumstances, we frown on the practice, my lord," Pratt said with a somber air of agreement. "The practice is underhanded at best."

"Then why did you sell my debt?" John demanded, flashing from dread to anger to fear.

Pratt shrugged, spreading his hands to the sides. "It was an offer I was not in a position to refuse."

"What on earth does that mean?" John asked, more alarmed than ever.

"There were extenuating circumstances, my lord," Pratt said. "Circumstances that confidentiality agreements prevent me from elaborating on."

"This is preposterous," Harrison snapped. "Do you know who we are? Do you know who are friends are? Lord Clerkenwell himself is a close associate of ours."

John held out a hand to steady Harrison, though he felt like shouting the same things himself. He swallowed again, took a deep breath, then asked, "Who has purchased my debt?"

"I am not at liberty to say, my lord," Pratt said.

"Not at liberty to say?" Harrison gaped, throwing up his hands.

Pratt glanced to him, then back at John. "All I can say is that the party in question has plans to contact you very soon."

"That is all you can say?" John had an exceedingly bad feeling about the situation.

"That is all, my lord, I swear it," Pratt confirmed. "My wellbeing is at risk here as well."

That comment settled it. Pratt must have sold his debt to a criminal, someone so dubious that he couldn't even mention his name. The bastard must have had shady dealings of his own with whoever it was that made it impossible to even speak the name.

"I guess that is the end of our association, then," John managed to croak. He glanced to Harrison. "We should be going."

"We should be wringing this man's neck," Harrison argued.

John shook his head and practically pushed Harrison out of the office. "We need to come up with a course of action," he said as they made their way out of the office. "And if I'm smart, I need to find the money as soon as possible."

More, if his suspicions were correct. Having one's debt purchased generally meant that debt would increase at an exponential rate. There was no telling how much he would owe, before all was said and done. There was no telling how, or even whether, he would make it out of the alarming new situation in one piece.

CHAPTER 6

or the next few days, John could hardly keep a single thought in his head. He'd spent hours discussing the problem of his purchased debt with his man of business, Mr. Fellowes, looking for a solution that would satisfy the mysterious new entity to whom he owed money without bankrupting the estate he'd inherited or selling off anything that would inconvenience his mother or Diana. Indeed, he and Fellowes scrambled to find ways to avoid letting John's mother or Diana know there was a problem at all.

At first, Fellowes seemed to have found a solution. He'd found a way for John to sell a few prize horses and to divide up and sell a portion of his country estate that would cover the debt while being as unobtrusive as possible. But only a day after coming up with the plan, Fellowes backed out of it.

"It wouldn't be prudent at this time, my lord," he

explained to John on the third morning after John's nerve-wracking meeting with Pratt. The expression Fellowes wore as he stood before the desk in John's office was odd at best, and it agitated John to no end.

"Not prudent?" John gaped at him, fidgeting in his seat. "Fellowes, just yesterday you told me this was a brilliant plan, that it would provide the needed funds, and that my mother and wife would be none the wiser."

"I...er...have received additional information about the...um...nature of the situation," Fellowes said. The man grasped his hands behind his back, and if John didn't know better, he would have thought the blighter was trying not to smile, of all things.

"You think I'm a fool for getting myself into this situation." John frowned at the man. "That's why you're laughing at me."

Fellowes immediately cleared his throat and schooled his expression. "I can assure you, I would never laugh at you, my lord. These sorts of unfortunate investments happen to the best of men." His mouth twitched with mirth for a moment before he cleared his throat again and sobered.

John let out an exasperated breath and pushed a hand through his hair. He was on the verge of giving Fellowes a piece of his mind, if only to relieve some of the tension roiling through him, when Diana walked past his study door. She walked slowly and cast a sideways look into the room, almost as though she wanted to listen in on the meeting. For a fleeting second, John thought his bride sent Fellowes a clever look. But no, why would Diana know Fellowes from a shrub in Hyde Park?

"Diana," he called out all the same, jumping up from his desk and heading for the hall. "Do excuse me, Fellowes. I wish to spend a bit of time with my bride."

"Understandable, my lord." Fellowes smiled outright.

The irrational worry that Fellowes had his sights set on Diana struck John for a moment before he shook it away. "Keep working on our dilemma, Fellowes," he charged the man as he walked out of his study.

He picked up his pace, catching Diana at the end of the hall as she turned into the morning parlor.

"You're looking beautiful this morning," he told Diana with a genuine smile.

Diana paused just inside of the parlor and glanced back at him with a flush of surprise. "You really think so? Wearing this old thing?"

She glanced down at the simple morning outfit she wore. John swept her with a look as well, practically vibrating with unfulfilled lust. She wore a simple blouse of some lightweight material. It had a high collar to which she'd affixed a brooch that appeared to be made of sapphire. It couldn't have been real, of course, but it brought out the blue in her eyes. Her skirt was of a simple, narrow style as well and hugged her hips in the most enticing way, creating elegant lines that made Diana look like the fashion plate she should be. Diana's blonde hair was caught up in an elegant but simple style that matched her clothing, but she wore sapphire drop earrings—which, again, couldn't have possibly been real—to match her brooch.

"You always were the most beautiful woman I've ever known," John said, alarmed at how much of a lovesick schoolboy he sounded. But it was true. Diana was heavenly.

And if he didn't do something to smooth things over between the two of them and bring Diana to the point where she wanted him as much as he wanted her, he might not last through a single month of marriage. Sleeping in a bed next to the woman was proving to be torture, considering that she was bound and determined to shut him out. She had every right to, of course, but damn if he didn't wish for a way to break through her resistance.

"Thank you, John," she said, arching one eyebrow and walking deeper into the room. She reached a sofa near one of the room's tall windows, light streaming through it, and took up a book that was resting on the seat. With all the grace of the queen, she sat and arranged herself artistically on the sofa, then opened the book.

Only when John realized he'd been watching her like she was on stage did he shake himself and move forward. "Aren't you going out with your friends today to pay calls?" he asked.

She glanced slowly up at him, fire and mischief in her eyes. "Today is my day to be at home," she said.

"Oh." He moved even closer to the sofa, hesitated, then sat by her side. She went back to reading, but he couldn't leave things there. "Should you be reading when people come to call on you?"

Again, she lifted her gaze to meet his. This time there were spikes mingled in the heat of her gaze. "Frankly, I am not expecting anyone to call on me. Oddly enough, I am not considered the sort of woman high society ladies care to visit anymore."

Guilt like nothing John had ever known lashed him. "I'm so sorry, Diana, you know I am." He scooted closer to her on the sofa. "If I could take back my behavior and do it all over again, you know I would."

"Would you?" She arched one eyebrow at him and closed her book with a decided snap. "Would you have behaved any differently? You have behaved like a perfect monster to me for years. Why should I believe you would change your ways now?"

"Because I see the truth of how I was and who I used to be," he admitted in a rush. "Because I now know it was terribly irresponsible of me to vex you so when all I really wanted to do—" He stopped and let out a heavy breath. Her eyes told him that she wasn't buying a word of his flowery speech.

He changed tactics, flopping against the back of the sofa. "Oh, come off it, Diana. You know that you enjoyed our games as much as I did."

Whether that was the right thing to say or not, it piqued Diana's interest. She stiffened and turned to him, a downright terrifying light in her eyes. "You think I enjoyed being made the brunt of jokes and an object of laughter for two years?"

"It was fun," John said with a shrug. "And you got in as many good hits as I did."

"Did I?" she asked with a tight jaw. A deeper sort of cleverness filled her eyes, making them sparkle like the jewels she wore.

"That is to say, your pranks were never quite as good as mine." John sent her the sauciest grin he could muster, under the circumstances, intentionally trying to get under her skin. Lord, but he would love to do more than just get under her skin.

Diana laughed, the sound almost cruel. "You are more of a simpleton than I thought if you think you've bested me."

"Haven't I?" John sat straighter, leaning toward her. "I got you to marry me, after all."

Her brow shot up. "Is that what those years of torture were intended to do? Get me to marry you?"

"Of course." John shrugged, grinning like the devil. He inched a hand closer to her leg, calculating the movements it would take to sweep her into his arms and twist her to lay her across the sofa. If no one was planning to call, he could have his way with her right there in the parlor.

"If you wanted to marry me, you should have just proposed, you fool." Diana tilted her chin up and crossed her arms. "You could have saved both of us time and trouble."

"But there would have been no fun in that at all," John argued. Better to use that excuse, rather than confessing that money had kept them apart so long.

"You have an odd definition of fun, my lord," she told him with a frosty sniff.

"Do I?" He saw his opening and prepared to take it. "And I suppose you don't think this is fun."

Before she could reply, he pounced, scooting closer to her and slipping his arms around her. He leaned in, capturing her mouth with his own. The kiss took her by surprise, which gave him the upper hand. He molded his lips to hers, tasting and teasing them. As he did, he stroked one hand along her side while balancing her in his arms with the other. She made a sound that might have been a protest or a sigh of longing. He chose to take it as the latter and brushed his tongue along the seam of her lips.

She parted those soft lips for him with a gasp, and he thrust his tongue alongside hers. The effect was magical. For a moment, Diana tensed, then she let every ounce of that tension drain from her body as she kissed him back. Her mouth was suddenly as hungry as his, exploring and devouring him with a strength that had his prick standing up and taking notice. She closed her arms around him as well, gripping the muscles of his back as if she liked what she had in her hands.

It was the most glorious moment of hope John had had all week. His worries scattered, and all he could think about were his chances of convincing her to abandon the parlor and the callers that weren't coming to rush upstairs with him. He would adore making love to her for the first time in the morning. The bright sunlight would mean he could see every bit of her and she could see him.

He was seconds away from raising the possibility with her when the sound of a throat clearing from the parlor doorway shook him. All of John's tension returned as she snapped straight, panting, and twisted to see who had the nerve to interrupt them.

"My lord," his butler, Merriweather, said, looking highly embarrassed. "An urgent letter has come for you."

Annoyance pulsed through John, especially when Diana scrambled away from him, her face pink and her breath coming in shallow gasps. She sat straight and did her best to appear prim and proper. John considered it a great loss.

"Merriweather, I don't know if you can see, but now is not exactly a time for delivering letters," John snapped.

"This one is desperate, my lord," Merriweather said, avoiding meeting John's eyes.

"You'd better see what it is, then," Diana said in a breathless voice.

John sighed and stood, keenly aware of his tented trousers. There was nothing to do but pretend everything was normal, even though it was as far from normal as possible. He marched across the room to snatch the letter from Merriweather's hand. The butler immediately retreated as John stomped back to the center of the room, ripping open the envelope and yanking out the letter inside.

As soon as he read it, every bit of his anger and his arousal vanished.

"*Dear Lord Whitlock,*" the letter read. "*The time has come for you to pay for your indiscretions. I have purchased your debt in full from Mr. Pratt. It is now I whom you owe for your mistakes and your sins. Meet me at the attached address on Friday afternoon at one o'clock.*" The letter was simply sighed, "*DD, LW.*"

John swallowed hard and read the letter over three more times. His chest felt so tight that he couldn't take in a full breath. Visions of what the man who had sent the letter wanted to talk about filled his head. He imagined meeting the bastard in a dark room. The bloke would probably be seated behind an impossibly huge desk with hulking bodyguards on either side of him. John imagined the man with a toothy grin and a deep, menacing laugh. The situation in his head was one he wasn't certain he'd be able to get out of in one piece.

"What is it?" Diana asked, blinking rapidly as she sat on the sofa. Her expression was odd, as if she couldn't decide whether to be sober or merry. John knew full well her reaction was because of his kiss and the way Merriweather had interrupted her. He shouldn't have taken her by surprise like that.

"It's nothing," he said, beginning to pace when he noticed his hands shaking.

He reread the letter for a fourth time, narrowing his

eyes at the odd signature. Were those the initials of the man he now owed? DD and LW? Were they two men or was the second part a title of some sort? He didn't recognize the abbreviation as anything associated with the medical profession or as any sort of honorific awarded to a knight. Could it be a location? London West? If so, that was an unusual way to phrase things.

"Really, John," Diana said, sounding put out as she rose from the sofa. "I can tell it's not nothing. Let me see the letter." She held out her hand as she walked toward him.

"No." He snatched the letter away from her, pressing it to his chest to keep her from seeing its contents. "That is, er, I wouldn't want to trouble you with business."

Diana sent him a flat look. "Perhaps if you had been honest with me from the start and troubled me with your business, we wouldn't be in the predicament we're in now."

"This sort of thing is not for the faint of heart," John insisted, marching away from her. He refolded the letter and crammed it back into its envelope.

"When have you ever known me to be faint of heart?" she asked, standing tall and facing him with strength.

John sighed, dropping his shoulders. "In truth, never," he admitted. "Not only are you the most beautiful woman I've ever known, you are the strongest. And, dare I say, the cleverest."

She wasn't impressed by his flattery. "Then stop being such a squirrel and show me that letter."

"A squirrel?" John straightened, smiling in spite of himself. "Me?"

"You're certainly behaving as one," Diana pointed out. "The nervous movements, the way you're trying to tuck that letter away." Indeed, he was slipping it into the interior pocket of his jacket as they spoke. "Everything about you has been anxious and squirrelish these last few days. Indeed, the comparison to nuts is irresistible." Her mouth twitched into a grin and her eyes flashed with impishness.

John laughed in spite of himself. "I have done you enough harm already, my dear, sweet bride," he said walking across the room to her. "It is my fondest wish now to spare you from any further hardship because of my foolish actions."

"Oh, so you're admitting that you've performed foolish actions you have yet to tell me about?" she asked, crossing her arms.

John had the feeling she'd crossed her arms deliberately to prevent him from embracing her. "It's not something you need to worry about. All you should concern yourself with is our earlier activity and ways we might extend it to fill the morning, since you are under the impression that society no longer wants you." He played his trump card by gazing heatedly into her eyes and saying, "I want you."

Her lips twitched as her gaze fixed on his mouth. Her porcelain skin flushed with desire. The heat in her eyes was unmistakable. For a few, blessed seconds, John was convinced she was going to give in to him at last. She even leaned forward, bringing her lips to within inches of his.

But then she whispered, "Not until you treat me in the manner in which I deserve to be treated."

She backed away, the spark in her eyes enough to light the whole room on fire. She turned, and with a final glance at John over her shoulder, she sashayed out of the room, leaving him alone and pulsing with unspent desire.

CHAPTER 7

*I*n spite of the imperious air Diana fought to maintain, she could feel her heart melting. John might have been a flirt and a bounder, but in the days since their hasty wedding, after spending so much time with him on such a close level, Diana was beginning to see that he had a good heart under his brazen exterior. Of course, she'd known that all along. She wouldn't have stood for his teasing if she hadn't felt it on some level. But living with him and seeing him tie himself in knots trying to make things right with her and hide the full extent of his troubles was endearing. And his kisses were fiery.

Friday couldn't come soon enough, as far as she was concerned. After the kiss in the parlor, she knew that her resistance was crumbling. She wanted far more kisses from him. She wanted to reach for him when they shared a bed at night and feel the full force of his passion. She wanted to give herself to him in every way imaginable and learn how to get as much as she gave. But she wasn't willing to do that until after she'd won their years long battle of wits.

Which was why she was relieved beyond measure when Friday finally arrived.

"I'm lunching with Bea today," she informed John after breakfast. "Which means I need to leave the house at eleven to meet her."

"Oh." John seemed genuinely disappointed. "I was hoping we might have lunch together." He fiddled anxiously with his watch fob for a moment. "I have an important business meeting this afternoon, and I thought lunch with you would give me the courage to face it."

Diana arched an eyebrow at him. "What sort of business meeting?"

"It's nothing you need to trouble yourself over," he said in a rush.

It was all Diana could do not to huff with impatience. She'd given him more than enough clues in the last few days for him to puzzle out that she was the one who had purchased his debt and sent the note. She'd even signed the note with her own initials, Diana Darrow, Lady Whitlock. John hadn't deciphered her rather obvious clue, and he was being a dolt about the whole thing now.

"Enjoy your meeting on your own, then," she said in clipped tones, tilting her chin up and marching past him to fetch her coat and hat.

As she walked across the square to fetch Bea—who was determined to be in on the prank—Diana shook her head in frustration. John was the author of his own troubles. It was a good thing she'd married him after all. She had the feeling she would keep him out of a great deal of trouble in the future. That was, when she wasn't the source of his trouble.

"Mr. Piper said he would meet us at the rented office," Diana told Bea as they walked across the square toward the city. More than a few of the inhabitants of the square and beyond sent Diana sidelong looks before falling into whispers with each other. Diana tried to keep her head held high, but the slights she had received every day since the May Flowers tableau continued to sting.

"Mr. Piper is the actor, correct?" Bea asked, her eyes bright with mischief.

"He is," Diana said with a nod. "He comes highly recommended. Apparently, he's a friend of Lady Phoebe's husband, Danny Long. Mr. Long assured me that Mr. Piper is not only talented, he is discreet as well."

"Do you have the lines you need him to learn?" Bea asked as they dodged a pair of nannies pushing prams. Bea grinned fondly at them and pressed a hand to her stomach.

Diana felt a swoop of expectation in her gut. All it would take for her to end up in the same condition as her friends was a crook of her finger in John's direction. But she wasn't going to give in until she saw her prank to its conclusion.

"I have the lines right here," Diana said with a wicked grin, patting the purse she carried. "If Mr. Piper is as accomplished as I've been told he is, he should be able to deliver the message I want John to hear with all the gravitas necessary."

Bea glanced sideways at her. "You aren't really going to frighten him, are you?"

Diana's grin widened. "Whether John is frightened or not will be entirely on him. If his imagination runs away with the things I plan to instruct Mr. Piper to say, then that is his responsibility, not mine."

Bea looked uncertain, but Diana was confident her plot would succeed.

The office she'd hired for the prank was in a nondescript building near the edge of the city. The building contained the offices of several solicitors and men of business. The office directly across the hall on the ground floor was marked as the Law Office of Dandie & Wirth. Mr. Piper had suggested the location himself, claiming he knew Mr. Wirth and his secretary, Mr. Mercer, personally. A few more questions had revealed that the Mr. Mercer in question was the brother of Mr. Phineas Wirth, who had recently married Diana and Bea's friend, Lenore Garrett. To Diana, that was a good sign. She was certain her plan would work.

"Do you understand what I'm asking of you, Mr. Piper?" she asked once she and Bea and Mr. Piper had arranged the office the way Diana wanted it.

"Absolutely," Mr. Piper said, glancing over the sheets of dialog and potential responses Diana had given him to learn. "I must say, Lady Whitlock, I admire your pluck. Lord Whitlock is a lucky man."

"Lord Whitlock is a jackanapes who is about to get what he deserves," Diana replied, hands on her hips.

"I can see that," Mr. Piper chuckled, continuing to study his lines. He paused and glanced up at Diana. "Tell me, just how desperate do you want me to make him? I could have him quivering in his boots, if you'd like."

Considering Mr. Piper's jolly demeanor, Diana wasn't certain she believed him. The man radiated good nature and fun. "I want him terrified," she said, assuming that if a jovial man like Mr. Piper aimed for terror, he might hit the right level of concern that Diana required.

"Right you are," Mr. Piper said with a wink. "Lordy, but this will be fun."

As one o'clock approached, Diana and Bea took their places, concealing themselves behind a bookshelf that had been positioned in such a way to hide one entire side of the room. Additionally, Mr. Piper had come up with an ingenious system of mirrors that would allow Diana to scribble additional notes or feed him new lines as the conversation with John progressed. A framed mirror on the desk—which would appear as nothing more than a framed picture to anyone standing in front of the desk— had been rigged to reflect the gap between the bookshelf and the wall, where Diana would be concealed. As far as Diana was concerned, being able to suggest new lines to Mr. Piper as the meeting progressed was a coup.

Finally, at one o'clock precisely, a knock on the door

announced John's arrival. Diana and Bea clapped hands over their mouths to hide their excited giggles.

"Come in," Mr. Piper called in a voice that was astoundingly dark and unlike the tones he'd used with them.

Diana's eyes went wide and her heart raced so fast she felt faint for a moment as John entered the office.

"Lord Whitlock," Mr. Piper said, adjusting the way he sat behind the desk so that he seemed to grow to twice his size. Diana could see his face reflected in the mirror on the desk and nearly gasped at how effectively he was able to change his entire countenance from the jolly man they'd discussed the plan with to a glowering man of business. "Come in," Mr. Piper continued in a voice that gave Diana chills. Perhaps she shouldn't have told him to be so terrifying after all.

"Good afternoon, sir." John took a few steps into the room, shut the door behind him, then stepped closer to the desk. He removed his hat and spun it anxiously in his hands. "I'm sorry, I don't know how to address you. Your letter contained only initials."

"You may address me as sir," Mr. Piper said, rising halfway out of his chair, planting his hands on the desk, and scowling at John.

Diana could only barely see John through slats in the false bookshelf that were designed to appear as the spines of books to anyone in the room. She would have given anything for a better view of his face, which was currently creased with concern.

John cleared his throat and took another step toward the desk. "Am I correct in assuming, sir, that you are the one who has purchased my debt from Mr. Pratt?"

Mr. Piper resumed his seat. He leaned back, taking his time before answering, "Yes. It is I to whom you now owe a shocking amount of money."

Diana bit her lip, thrilled that Mr. Piper was proving to be worth the amount she was paying him.

John cleared his throat and shifted anxiously. "You wished to speak to me about it, and I can only assume that you intend to share your terms of repayment."

"You are correct," Mr. Piper said. "But first, we must discuss the debt itself."

"Sir?" John swallowed hard. He was trying his best to maintain an air of strength in the face of the fear Mr. Piper was attempting to instill in him. Diana was impressed by that much. A lesser man would be trembling in his boots, what with the way Mr. Piper was throwing his all into the charade.

"How does a man of your breeding and education find himself fifty thousand pounds in debt?" Mr. Piper asked, giving John his most intimidating look.

Some of the color drained from John's face. "I believe my debt is only thirty thousand, sir."

Mr. Piper chuckled with such menace that it made the hair on the back of Diana's neck stand up. Perfect.

"We will discuss the amount in a moment," Mr. Piper said, just as Diana had instructed. "What I would like to know is how a man like you finds himself in such financial straits."

"It was not intentional, I can assure you," John said, letting out a breath. He shoved a hand through his hair before going on. "I inherited the Whitlock estate and finances from my father several years ago and was alarmed by the state things were in. As you may know, all across England, the older estates are having trouble adjusting to the new economy. It was suggested that I marry an American heiress or some other woman who would bring a fortune with her—"

Diana gasped. She hadn't known John had been pressured to marry for money.

"—but I simply couldn't," he went on. "You see, I've been in love with the same woman for years, since the moment I met her."

Diana pressed a hand to her chest. Her heart began beating so furiously that she feared it could be heard from her hiding place.

"How does a man bankrupt himself for love?" Mr. Piper asked, ad libbing, but keeping well within character.

John shrugged, opening his hands in a gesture of surrender. "At first, it was merely an effort to improve the finances of my family's estate. I saw quickly that improvements wouldn't be possible without an infusion of capital. So I sought out investments to make up what our bank balance lacked."

"I take it those investments were not successful?" Mr.

Piper said, continuing to ad lib. He glanced at Diana through the mirrors, as if seeking her approval.

Diana nodded. She gestured for Bea to hand her the slate and chalk they had with them, in case she needed to change the script for the encounter.

John went on. "As it happened, I was given bad investment advice." He sighed, his posture sagging. "I should have known better than to speculate on resources. That first loss was a hard one to bear. I did try to make up for it, though."

"Did you?" Mr. Piper steepled his fingers and frowned darkly at John. He checked in the mirror as well. Again, Diana nodded in encouragement and approval.

"I made some of that loss back," John went on. "But by that point, I was head over heels in love with Diana. That is, Lady Whitlock."

Diana quickly scribbled on her slate, then held it up at the right angle for Mr. Piper to see. Mr. Piper pretended to nod sagely as he checked in the mirror. He adjusted slightly so that he could read what Diana had written, which must have appeared backwards to him.

Finally, after what seemed like a glaringly suspicious pause, Mr. Piper asked as Diana had directed, "Why didn't you simply marry Lady Diana for her money?"

"Everyone said I should," John answered with a guilty look. "But I couldn't do that to her. I've loved Diana for years, you see. I couldn't bear what she would have thought of me if she'd learned I proposed because I needed the money from her dowry to save my neck."

Diana's heart squeezed in her chest. At least, for a moment. After her initial bout of affection and sentiment, old resentment swooped back in. She erased her previous message on the slate with the side of her hand, wrote a new one, then held it up for Mr. Piper to read.

"You could have discussed the matter with the lady," Mr. Piper delivered the message, then elaborated perfectly. "You could have asked her what she thought of using the money she brought with her into marriage instead of assuming she would be upset. Isn't that what women have been fighting for all this time? The right to have their voices heard?"

God bless Mr. Piper and his forward-thinking attitude, Diana thought to herself. The man was far more of a genius than her first impression of him had hinted at.

"I can see now that I should have consulted her," John said, shaking his head. "But that's all water under the bridge now. What's done is done. I've humiliated her into marriage—something I will regret every day for the rest of my life—"

"You regret marrying the woman you love?" Mr. Piper asked, breaking character slightly.

Diana held her breath, slate poised in front of her, but with no idea what to write.

"I don't regret it for a moment," John said. He hesitated, then let his shoulders drop as he answered, "That is to say, I regret not asking her sooner. I should have married Diana years ago. She's the most wonderful creature in the world. But I didn't think I deserved her, you see. Not with the financial hole I kept digging deeper and deeper."

Diana clenched her jaw. Of all the damn foolish, overly sentimental, uselessly maudlin things for John to feel. As much as it touched her to know he was a noble fool after all, it frustrated her that he hadn't simply been straight with her from the start. She scribbled a message to Mr. Piper to get on with things, then held the slate up.

Mr. Piper nodded. "It seems I am now the owner of that hole," he said. He shifted in his chair, then continued with the script Diana had planned earlier. "Here are my terms for the repayment of your debt."

John perked up. "Anything," he said. "I will work with you to find the most expedient way possible to pay back the money I owe."

"Any man who is foolish enough to find himself in so much debt shouldn't be trusted to find more money to pay it back," Mr. Piper recited. Diana wondered at the continuity of that line, considering how the conversation had gone, but it didn't seem to matter. "And so, in lieu of a cash payment, Lord Whitlock, I will allow you to repay me by handing over the most precious thing you own."

"I beg your pardon?" John blinked at Mr. Piper.

Diana grinned from ear to ear, eager to watch the twist in her plot unfold. The whole thing was designed to twist John into knots more than to worsen his financial situation.

"You heard me," Mr. Piper continued, back to being utterly terrifying. "I want the most precious thing you own as payment. And don't think to cross me or attempt to fool me. I'll know if the thing you offer me is truly your most valuable possession or if you are trying to wiggle out of your sins."

Diana held her breath, waiting to see what John would come up with. She was certain he would offer the gold pocket watch John's father had given him on his deathbed. She already had visions of herself surprising John with the watch and earning his eternal admiration and thanks that it hadn't been taken from him after all.

But John surprised her by saying, "The most valuable thing I have or that I could ever have is my wife, sir."

Diana blinked, holding her breath. Her heart throbbed against her ribs.

"Diana is everything to me. I could be a pauper and count myself the luckiest man in the world if I still had her. I will give you every possession I own, my house, my land, and every ounce of respect that goes with it. But if you want the most valuable thing I have, well, that is Diana. And I would not give her to you, even if it meant my death."

A dead silence filled the room. Diana blinked back tears of sentiment that shocked her to her core. She'd figured John loved her. Any man who had gone through what he had for her must love her on some level. But she'd had no idea that love was so potent or so pure.

Mr. Piper cleared his throat, snapping Diana back to attention. To John, he must have looked as though he were thinking things over. In fact, he was staring desperately into the mirror, as if asking Diana how she wanted to proceed.

Diana thought as fast as she could, writing on the slate with a shaking hand.

"I need time to think about this," Mr. Piper delivered her line. "I cannot accept a wife as payment, but there must be some sort of reckoning." Again, he was making up his own lines, but Diana approved. "Come back on Monday, and I will tell you what the price of your foolishness will be."

John looked confused—and a bit humbled—but he nodded and took a step back. "Thank you, sir. I will return on Monday."

A few seconds of hesitation followed as John bowed a second time. He looked as though he would say more, but in the end, he left without another word. Not once did he look at the bookshelf, or any other part of the room. Diana was reasonably certain that he didn't have the first clue who was really behind the meeting.

Once John shut the door behind him, Martin got up from the desk and rushed to lock it. "It's safe to come out, my lady," he said.

Diana and Bea climbed out from behind the bookshelf, confident John wouldn't barge in and discover the whole thing.

"Well," Bea said, holding a hand to her chest and fanning her red-rimmed eyes with the other. "If that was not the most romantic thing I've ever heard, I don't know what is."

Diana grinned at her friend. "Romantic? For a man to lose all his money rather than simply talking to the woman he loves to see if they can come up with a solution together?"

"You have to admit," Mr. Piper said, fully returned to his affable self, "it was rather romantic."

"All right," Diana conceded with a laugh. "It was romantic. But it wasn't good enough for me to bring the whole thing to an end yet."

"It wasn't?" Bea blinked at her.

"John was clearly sorry that he lost the money, but I'm not convinced he's sorry he didn't seek my help and advice earlier," Diana explained.

"Yes, I was wondering about that myself," Mr. Piper said. "You would think that even a man as steeped in tradition as a viscount would concede that the world is changing and that women should have a part in matters of their own estate. Assuming he planned to marry you and make that estate yours from the start, as it seemed to me he did. If Parliament can pass laws giving women those responsibilities, then men should give them as well."

"Why, Mr. Piper," Diana smiled. "I had no idea you were so advanced in your beliefs."

"Believe me, my lady," Mr. Piper said with a wink, "it behooves me to be as progressive in my thinking as possible."

Diana couldn't quite puzzle out what he meant by

that, but she didn't need to. Her plan was already veering off in a different direction in her mind.

"I'll give John one more chance to come to me for financial advice. If he sees the light and decides to make this my problem, as his wife, as much as his own, then I'll reveal all to him," she said. "If not, I have one last prank to play. If that doesn't make him see the light, then nothing will."

CHAPTER 8

*J*ohn hadn't thought it was possible to feel both panic and relief at the same time. He'd left the office of his creditor—he still didn't know the man's name, which was a horrible oversight on his part—roiling with dread. The man was intimidating, he had to admit. And he seemed to know far more about him than John was comfortable with. Asking for the most precious thing he owned as compensation for the debt was clearly a move to put John in his debt forever. Untangling the mess he'd made through bad investments was going to be so much harder than John had imagined.

And yet, he'd also left the office with the feeling that he could do it. The mysterious creditor would let him come up with payment, and if John played his cards right, he would forgive the debt entirely. All John had to do was come up with enough money—and something that was dear to him as a token—and he could make things right. He was certain of it.

He had to make things right. Far more than just his life depended on it. That fact was driven home to him the next morning, when Diana appeared in the doorway of his office as he was rifling through drawers, scouring cabinets, and turning over everything in search of bank books, deeds, and anything else that could serve as collateral for the repayment of his debt.

"Good heavens, John. What are you doing?" Diana asked, snapping John's attention away from his search.

She was lovely. That was all there was to it. That morning, she was dressed in an elegant walking dress that highlighted the curve of her hips and the swell of her breasts. Her golden hair was styled in a cascade of curls atop her head with a small hat affixed to the whole thing, as if she had plans to go out. But it was her face that caught John's attention more than anything else. In spite of all her disappointments and set-backs—disappointments he'd caused—her cheeks glowed with health and her blue eyes sparkled with life and wit.

It took several seconds for John to realize he was merely staring at her, the papers in his hands sagging, as if he might drop them. "You are the most beautiful creature God ever created," he said, letting his words come out with a reverence he would have tried to hide from her before.

Diana's lips pulled into a sly grin as she took a few slow steps into his office, her body swaying enticingly as she did. "What torment are you planning for me now that requires such flattery to throw me off-guard?"

John swallowed the lump of guilt in his throat. "I swear, Diana, I'm not flattering you as a way to tease you. I genuinely believe you are amazing." To prove it, he set the papers he'd been sorting through aside and crossed the room to her.

Before she could protest, he slipped his hands around her narrow waist and tugged her close. Diana was too surprised by the gesture to flinch or fight back as he slanted his mouth over hers, stealing a kiss that came straight from his heart.

His worried, wounded heart. What had he done to her? Not only had he behaved like a cad for years, his precarious financial situation was insult added to every injury he'd inflicted. He owed her so much. He owed her a happy and secure life.

A newfound determination filled him as he broke their kiss, leaning away to study her face. "I swear to you, Diana, I am going to make you the happiest woman in England, the happiest woman in the world."

Diana's startled—and aroused—look melted slowly to a different sort of surprise. "Well," she breathed out, placing a hand over her heart as she inched out of his embrace. "Isn't that a promise."

"It's a promise I should have made long ago," John said definitively. "And as soon as I get a few things in order, it's a promise I intend to fulfill."

A curious expression came over Diana's flushed face.

"And what sort of things do you need to get in order?" she asked, arching one eyebrow.

John opened his mouth, but pride stopped him from saying anything. He couldn't burden Diana with the truth. She already had far too much to deal with. As he understood it, society was holding fast in their determination to snub her after the ruinous scene at the May Flowers tableau. Women took great stock in their reputations, and he was certain Diana needed every bit of her powers of concentration to reclaim her place at the height of London's finest social circles.

"It's nothing you need to worry about," he told her with an adoring smile. He leaned toward her and stole another kiss before peeling away and returning to his desk.

Diana remained silent, and when he glanced up at her, he was alarmed to find her face pinched with frustration. "You can share your troubles with me, John," she insisted. "I am made of tough stuff. And I might even have a solution for you."

John winced, feeling the pull to confess all as keenly as ever.

Before he could say anything, Diana walked closer to the desk, holding out her hand. "Come. I'm going for a walk in Hyde Park and you're coming with me."

"Would that I had time," John gave his excuse with a sigh, glancing to the papers on his desk.

"You're coming with me," Diana said in a more forceful voice, clipping her words.

John glanced at her, his brow shooting up. He knew the look on her face. She wasn't going to back down until he agreed to go with her. The longer he prolonged things, the more she would dig in her heels.

He rubbed a hand over his face and made an impatient sound. "All right," he said. "But it will have to be a short walk. I have desperately important matters to deal with."

"What kind of desperately important matters?" Diana asked in her most wheedling tone as they headed out of the office and down the hall.

She was already dressed to go out, but John was spared coming up with an excuse not to talk about it as he searched for the right hat to wear for a walk in Hyde Park. He thought he'd successfully avoided the discussion entirely as they left the house and headed west through Mayfair.

At least until Diana repeated, "What matters are so desperately important that they have you turning your office inside out?"

"Truly, Diana, I don't wish to burden you with these cares," John replied, resting his free hand over her gloved one as it nestled in the crook of his elbow.

He could tell in an instant that was the wrong answer. "Are you going to make me guess?" she asked in a flat voice.

"I wish you wouldn't," John replied just as flatly.

As they continued on through the neighborhoods around their home, John became acutely aware of the stares and whispers that followed them. They were infuriating. He had thought that gossip and innuendo would die down once he and Diana were married. He'd thought that the modern world was beyond such things as displays of public shame, that those sorts of snubs were more suited to their grandparents' generation. He was aggravated to see those attitudes still existed. They fueled the protectiveness he felt for Diana, recharging his need to do whatever he could to be her champion.

"This is about money, isn't it?" Diana asked as they reached Hyde Park Corner and started down one of the lanes, through magnificent flower gardens.

John nearly missed a step. "What makes you think that?" he asked in a too-tight voice.

"It's always about money," Diana said with an offhand gesture. "Money is the one thing that can turn a grown man's knees to jelly and make him turn his office upside down." She shot him a pointed sideways look.

"That's not true," he said, scrambling for a way to hide his folly. "Men get that way about women as well. And war. Which are nearly the same thing, if you ask me."

Diana laughed aloud at his quip, which went a long way to making John feel better. "Believe me, women see it as a war as well. But it is a war we're winning."

It was John's turn to laugh. "Don't be too sure about that." When she looked at him in a way that was almost offended, he went on with, "Women may be making unprecedented strides in fields such as education and work, but I doubt it will go so far as to gain your lot the vote or seats in government."

As he'd hoped, Diana's whole countenance lit as though he'd taken a match to kindling. "I thought you supported women's suffrage."

John made a noncommittal sound and scrunched his face as though he weren't sure.

"You beast." Diana swatted his arm. "You deceived me into believing you were more forward-thinking than this." She tilted her head up. "Mark my words. Someday, not only will women have the vote, the Prime Minister herself will be a woman."

John barked a laugh. "Not bloody likely. A woman should stay at home. That is her kingdom and her realm. That and motherhood, which should be your lot, but for the way you've been turning to ice at night."

"John!" Diana gasped, the fire of argument in her eyes. "You know full well that it is your—" She stopped abruptly, her mouth hanging open for a moment. A clever light came to her eyes, and she snapped her mouth shut. "You cannot distract me away from the topic at hand," she said, stopping and facing him halfway down the path that ran beside Carriage Drive. "You have money troubles, and it is time you stopped hiding them from me."

John fought not to flush at her shrewd observation, but it was a losing battle. "Whether I have money problems or not is none of your concern," he said. "I don't want you to worry about it."

A firm look turned her blue eyes to steel. "John, if you are in need of money, I wish you would ask me for it."

John laughed aloud. "And what good would that do? A lady's allowance is hardly enough to cover the debt I've accrued."

He cursed himself for letting the truth slip out the moment the words had passed his lips.

"Ask me for the money, John," Diana said, her jaw clenched and her eyes fierce.

"I couldn't possibly," he argued. "It would be a travesty. I'm not taking more from you than I already have."

Diana practically quivered with indignation. "Were you or were you not listening to the speech I gave the afternoon you ruined me entirely?"

John opened his mouth, but nothing came out at first. He sighed and rubbed a hand over his face. "Diana, women simply cannot handle money with any effectiveness. I know you believe that whatever sum you have acquired through your financial hobbies is impressive, but I can assure you, a few extra pounds of spending money cannot come anywhere close to the large sums that men deal with on a daily basis."

Diana's eyes widened in offense. "You think me incapable of understanding high finance? That the sums of money I have earned through my wits and my savvy are trifling?" Her voice shook with the question.

"Yes, darling." He attempted to take her hand, but she pulled away. "I am so proud of you for accomplishing what you have, but matters such as the one I find myself dealing with are for men to sort out. Women are simply incapable of comprehending the scope. And there's nothing wrong with that."

For a moment, John was certain Diana would strike him. She was that livid. Instead, she glanced back down Carriage Drive and nodded sharply.

John started to turn to see what she was nodding at, but she grabbed his attention by asking sharply, "Am I precious to you, John? Am I valuable?"

The question was so incongruous that John's mind stopped turning for a moment. "Yes, of course you are, darling." He reached for her hands again, but she took a large step back. "You are the most precious thing in the world to me, Diana." A familiar thought niggled at the back of his brain, but he couldn't focus on what it was. "I have been terribly remiss in telling you just how dear you are to me. I wasted years teasing you when I should have been making passionate love to you. I could say I'm sorry for the wasted time, and for the way I was instrumental in every unfortunate thing that has happened to you recently, but it would hardly make up for my sins. I love you."

For a moment, Diana's face softened, as though she were touched by his words. Too quickly, it pinched into a blend of frustration and hopelessness again. She glanced down Carriage Drive for a moment, then looked back to him. "I love you too, John. I always have. But you are the most vexing man in England. If you could only open your eyes and see things differently than you are determined to see them, every problem you've made for yourself would vanish. If you could just—"

Her words were cut off as a plain carriage came to an abrupt stop just behind her. She turned as the door opened and a burly man John had never seen before stepped down. The brute swooped toward Diana, throwing an arm around her. Diana let out a scream, then appeared to leap into the carriage along with the brute. A moment later, the carriage door slammed shut and the carriage rolled on.

The whole thing happened so fast that John didn't have time to react. He called out, "Diana!" and leapt after the carriage, but it was too late. All he could do was break into a run and attempt to chase the carriage as it rolled away.

"Diana!" he shouted again as he sprinted down Carriage Drive. Dozens of bystanders stopped what they were doing to watch the curious scene unfold, but none of them lifted a finger to help. Within seconds, the carriage had gained enough speed to get away, no matter how fast John ran. His lungs burned and his legs were on fire, but he kept running, knowing it was futile, until he tripped over his own feet and fell, sprawling across the gravel drive.

"My lord, my lord! Are you all right?" a young man called out behind him. He scurried the rest of the way to John, bending to help John to his feet.

"No," John panted. "I am not all right. My wife—"

He didn't know how to finish the sentence. He couldn't believe what had happened.

The young man's face was a mask of kind concern as he helped John brush dirt and gravel from his suit. There was something innocent in the lad's look. But the moment John was cleaned off and squared his shoulders as his mind raced to know what to do next, the lad's countenance changed entirely.

As if someone had lit a match, the young man was suddenly gruff. He scowled as he reached into his jacket and drew out a folded piece of paper. "I've been instructed to give this to you," he growled, thrusting the letter at John.

The whole thing was completely overwhelming. John took the paper, at a complete loss. The young man snarled at him, then turned and marched off. John gaped after him. It was almost as though the lad were part of some sort of play where he had a starring role as the villain.

There wasn't time to think about it. Drawing in a sharp breath, John opened the paper and read.

"I have what is most precious to you now. If you ever want to see your wife again, bring a diamond necklace, the deed to your London townhouse, and a box of chocolates to the Savoy Hotel, room 623, at eight o'clock tonight."

John's gut roiled as he stared at the note. It was utter madness. He was in so far over his head that he didn't think he would ever see the light of day again. Panting still from his run and his fall, he turned this way and that, glancing around him as if the answer to the madness his world had fallen into would appear at any second. But there was nothing.

"I have to do something," he told himself, reading the note again and again. "A box of chocolates?" His creditor was making fun of him now. The deed to the townhouse and a diamond necklace made sense, though. They were tangible items of financial value. And they were worthless trinkets that he would gladly part with if it meant getting Diana back.

But he wasn't ready to concede total defeat yet.

"Jack," he whispered to himself, hurrying back through Hyde Park to a corner where he would be able to hail a cab. He had to speak to Jack. As Assistant Commissioner of Scotland Yard, Jack would be able to call out the full force of the Metropolitan Police to help turn the city inside out in his search for Diana. He would find her, and he would find the bastard who had kidnapped her and make him pay.

CHAPTER 9

*J*ohn had run through every horrible scenario he could imagine in his head as he rode impatiently through the streets of London to Scotland Yard. He imagined Diana being manhandled, beaten, or worse. He would kill anyone who so much as dared to lay a finger on her. But at the same time, he cursed himself for letting things get so out of control.

Perhaps Diana was right. Perhaps he should have just swallowed his pride and consulted her on the entire situation. Even if she only had a few pounds to offer toward repaying his debt, since they were married, it was her debt as much as his now. And somewhere in the very back of his mind, a voice suggested that she might have more money than he assumed.

His thoughts were still swirling by the time he reached Scotland Yard, only to find that Jack wasn't in his office that day. He was at home. John was forced to hurry back out to the street to hail another cab, then to suffer through another interminable journey from Scotland Yard to Clerkenwell. His thoughts unraveled even more as he envisioned Diana chained and held captive, crying his name and begging for him to come rescue her. He still didn't know the name of the bastard who had taken her, but whoever the man was, he would pay.

"Jack, I need your help and I need it right now," John blurted as he burst into the well-appointed flat where he and Bianca lived.

Jack made quite a sight, standing in his shirtsleeves, holding his tiny son in one arm as he answered the door. He was disheveled and had a spit-up stain on one shoulder, but he'd never looked happier. "What the devil is the problem, man?" he asked as John pushed past him and began pacing around the room.

"Diana has been kidnapped," he said, practically throwing off his hat and raking his hands through his hair so hard it was a wonder he didn't pull great handfuls out.

"What?" Jack was instantly as alarmed as John was. "When was she taken and where? How did this happen? Is there a ransom note?"

His alarm was so sharp and came on so quickly that his son began to wail in his arms.

"What in heaven's name," Bianca said as she marched in from one of the back rooms. She went straight to Jack to take her son, which only freed Jack up to pace the room along with John. "What is going on here?"

"Diana has been kidnapped," John told her, scrambling for the most delicate way to tell Bianca. She was Diana's friend, after all. And as strong as they all knew she was, she was still a woman. Women were as likely as not to swoon upon hearing such news.

"Kidnapped?" Bianca asked with what John considered unnatural calm. She must not have understood the full reality of the situation.

"We were walking in Hyde Park," John told Jack. "We were having a discussion about...." Words failed him. Not all of his friends knew the full extent of his financial situation.

Jack, of course, picked up in an instant that John was holding back. "You have to tell me everything, man," he said, bristling with alarm and impatience. "Every little detail could be of vital importance. And tell me quickly. Time could be running out."

John swallowed, then reached into his pocket to take out the note the curious young man had delivered. As he handed it over to Jack, he said, "I owe money. A lot of money."

"How much?" Jack asked. He handed the note to Bianca almost absentmindedly.

John ran a hand over his face. "Thirty thousand pounds. Although it might be more now."

"Explain," Jack said in a harsh voice, scowling.

Behind him, Bianca made a sound. When John glanced in her direction, she clapped a hand to her mouth, almost as though she were trying to hide a grin.

"Nathan, you silly boy," she told her son, then marched away into one of the back rooms without further explanation.

John shook his head at the incongruous interruption, then turned back to Jack. "I owed the money to a Mr. Pratt, an investment broker. Thanks to his bad advice, I lost all that money speculating."

"He's the one who kidnapped Diana?" Jack looked ready to commit murder.

John shook his head. "No, Pratt visited me at the chapel shortly before the wedding, implying I should repay more of what I owed him. He probably heard about my marriage to Diana and came to inquire after her dowry. But the next day, when I went to him to make arrangements, Pratt informed me he'd sold my debt."

"Sold it?" Jack's dark look said he was well aware of everything that implied.

"I visited the new holder of the debt yesterday." He took a step toward Jack. "The man is a menace, clearly a criminal. He seemed more interested in turning the thumb screws than actually collecting the money. He asked for the most valuable thing I own as repayment, and, fool that I am, I told him Diana was my most precious possession. So he's taken her."

"We'll discuss your view of your wife as your possession later," Jack said, striding toward a hat stand by the door and grabbing his hat. "For now, we'll go to Scotland Yard and marshal all the resources we—"

"Jack!" Bianca interrupted him with a commanding

call. Both John and Jack turned to find her standing in the doorway with a peculiar look on her face. "Could I see you in private for a moment."

"John and I need to get to Scotland Yard," Jack argued, heading for the door. "Time is of the essence if we're to find Diana and rescue her."

"Now," Bianca ordered.

Jack stopped in mid stride. He glanced to John, then changed direction, crossing the room and disappearing into the back of the flat. Bianca shut the door behind them.

That left John alone with his thoughts, none of which were reassuring. He'd misspoken when he told Jack Diana was his possession. She most certainly wasn't. He could see that now more than ever. She was his heart, his life. She was the reason he wanted to wake up each day and everything he wanted to gather close to him in bed every night. He didn't know what he would do with himself if anything happened to her, if any harm came to her. He was a damned fool a thousand times over. Every second of every day that ticked by showed him that more and more. He didn't deserve Diana, but if he was lucky enough to get her back, he would endeavor to change that.

Several minutes ticked by before Jack stepped back into the main room. His expression was entirely transformed as he glanced at John. The alarm had completely vanished from his countenance. Instead of glittering with steely determination, the man's eyes danced with...

no, it couldn't be humor. John had to be seeing things wrong.

Jack cleared his throat. "Our first order of business should be procuring the items the kidnapper demanded in his ransom note. Do you have the funds to purchase a diamond necklace and a box of chocolates?" Jack's mouth twitched, as though he were fighting a grin.

"I can afford the chocolates," John said, striding over to where he'd tossed his hat on a side table, "but the necklace might be a problem." He put his hat on and marched with Jack to the door. Inspiration hit him once they reached the stairway leading down through Jack's building to the street. "My creditor seemed fixated with things that are precious to me, things with sentimental value. I could ask my mother for a diamond necklace, perhaps something that once belonged to her mother."

"Are you certain you wish to involve your mother in this?" Jack asked. His tone was far lighter than the alarm he had shown before. John was puzzled by it, but he hardly had time to dwell on Jack's behavior when Diana was the one who needed him.

"I'll tell her I wish to give it to Diana," John went on as they reached the street. Jack lifted a hand to hail a cab, and almost immediately, one swung by for them, proving just how important Jack was in his neighborhood. "Mama wanted me to go through her jewels to find some to bestow on Diana anyhow. I'm certain she'll allow me to take something."

Jack merely hummed in response, frowning deliberately.

The cab took them home to Mayfair by way of Oxford Street. John hopped out at a confectioner's shop while Jack waited with the cab. He purchased the first box of chocolates that the shopkeeper recommended to him, knowing he was being bilked by the exorbitant assortment. The chocolates were an insult, as like as not, so John didn't particularly care what sort they were.

From there, they continued on to Mayfair and home.

"But of course, I'll give you one of my necklaces," John's mother said with a smile as soon as John explained what he needed. "But darling, why the urgency? And why do you look as though you've seen a ghost? And where is Diana? I thought the two of you went for a stroll in Hyde Park."

John opened his mouth, but Jack interrupted with, "Perhaps I should explain to your mother while you—" He hesitated for a moment, then went on to say, "While you change into something more suitable for an evening out."

John gaped at him. "An evening out? I'm not going to the Savoy for a night on the town."

"Yes, but you don't want to draw suspicion once you arrive at the Savoy," Jack said.

It seemed like nonsense to John, but he trusted Jack's instincts on criminal matters more than his own. He raced upstairs and hurried to change. Haste made him clumsy, which made everything take longer.

By the time he was dressed and had caught up with Jack and his mother in her private sitting room, two of the upstairs maids were busy bringing in several loads of small boxes.

"Mama, what is all this?" John asked, surveying the clutter strewn all over the tables and chairs in the room.

"Do you know, my boy, I'm not certain where the necklace I feel I should give you is at the moment," his mother replied, far too much sparkle in her eyes. "We'll have to check each of these boxes that the girls have brought down from the attic one at a time."

It was the most maddening thing John had ever done in his life. Every minute that ticked by as they sorted through a lifetime of trinkets was agony. He kept picturing Diana in distress, needing him desperately. And here his mother seemed to find it necessary to tell every single story and recount every ball or soiree she'd attended in every piece of jewelry they unboxed.

"The Duke of Westmoreland asked me to dance that night," she giggled fondly over an exquisite diamond necklace that John was certain would meet his creditor's criteria, once they found it. "He wasn't the most charming of fellows, but he was a duke. And we were all mad for dukes back in those days."

"Yes, Mama, I'm certain you were." John roiled with impatience, glancing to the clock on his mother's mantel and practically dancing from foot to foot with impatience. The only thing that kept him from snatching the necklace right out of her hands and dashing out the door was that it wasn't yet eight o'clock. The hour was growing later and later, though. "We need to go," he told Jack—who seemed far, far too amused by his mother's reminiscences for a high-ranking police officer with a kidnapper to chase.

"We have time," Jack said, smiling indulgently at John's mother.

"I thought you said time was of the essence," John grumbled, stepping closer to him. He couldn't understand why everyone was so unconcerned with Diana's safety. Unless the ruination he'd caused had somehow made Diana not as valuable to even her own friends as she once was.

"The kidnapper gave you a time to meet him," Jack explained. "In my experience, rushing kidnappers who have allotted a specific time for negotiations could be disaster."

John growled in response. It didn't seem right. "Wouldn't it be better to get there early and catch him off-guard?"

Jack stared at him. "Who between us has more experience with law enforcement?"

John let out a breath. "You're right. I'll go down to my office and find the deed to this townhouse."

"Lord Clerkenwell, would you care to stay for supper?" John's mother asked.

"There isn't time, Mama," John nearly shouted.

Of all things, Jack looked like he might laugh. "Some

other time, Lady Whitlock." The man had the nerve to wink at his mother.

It was all completely and mind-numbingly mad. John managed to find the deed, but just as he and Jack were about to leave for the Savoy, his mother made a fuss about finding the appropriate box for the necklace. Once that was done, Jack had somehow misplaced the box of chocolates. John tried to leave for the Savoy without Jack and the chocolates, which led to a lecture from Jack in police procedure and hunting criminals.

By the time they finally did reach the Savoy, it was a few minutes past eight o'clock.

"So help me, Jack," John growled. "If the kidnapper has harmed a hair on Diana's head because of your delays, I'll murder you right along with him."

"You won't be able to help your dear wife from a prison cell," Jack chuckled as they approached the door to room six twenty-three. John turned to glare incredulously at the man. Jack cleared his throat and nodded to the door. "You'd best go in by yourself. I'll stand guard out here." He shoved the box of chocolates and the box containing the necklace at John.

John shuffled the two boxes in his arms and knocked on the door. Somewhere inside, a voice called back, "Come in."

With one final glance at Jack, John opened the door and stepped into the hotel room.

He was immediately on the alert. The room was dark, but for a small fire in the grate and a collection of candles placed throughout the room. It was a rather luxurious suite, complete with sofa, tables, and what looked like supper for two laid out near one of the curtained windows. A door at the far end of the room led to a bedroom, and standing in that doorway was a shadowy figure swathed in a black cloak.

"Where is my wife?" John demanded, marching toward the figure.

"Stop where you are," the figure demanded.

John could tell at once that it wasn't the man from the office, but he had no idea who else it could be. He stopped, but he couldn't keep still.

"I want my wife," he said in as strong a voice as he could manage. "If you've harmed so much as a hair on her head—"

The room door closed behind him with a loud clack. A moment later, a quieter click sounded as the door was locked from the outside. John jumped and twisted to see what had happened. How had Jack, of all people, let someone slip past him to trap him in the room.

"I take it you brought the items I requested?" the shadowy figure asked. There was something decidedly strange about his voice. It was deep, but high at the same time. Unlike a man at all.

"Tell me where Diana is," John demanded. "Unless you prove to me she is safe, I won't give you anything."

"I can assure you, she is safe," the shadowy figure said.

"Prove it."

For a split-second, John thought he heard an impatient sigh. The shadowy figure turned and gestured into the bedroom.

"I'm in here, John." Diana's voice sounded in the darkness. "Now do as you have been told."

John snapped his mouth shut, recoiling a bit at how irritated Diana sounded. He'd imagined she would be terrified and begging him to rescue her. Something wasn't right.

"What the devil is going on here?" he demanded, starting forward toward the bedroom.

"Stay right where you are," the shadowy figure ordered, turning back to him. "Show me what you've brought with you."

"Show me my wife. Show me that she is safe," John demanded right back.

"Not until I see the glitter of diamonds," the shadowy figure said. "Not until I smell the sweet scent of chocolate. Not until I see you are willing to give up your home to see your beloved Diana again."

John's back itched with agitation. Something wasn't right. No, strike that, everything wasn't right. The entire mood of the hotel room was off. Instead of feeling threatened and terrified, like ha had been all afternoon, he was merely aggravated. The whole situation was maddening instead of frightening. The kidnapper was toying with him instead of getting ready to cause him or Diana harm. He no longer felt as though his life or Diana's life were in danger, he merely felt frustrated.

He blinked. Frustrated, aggravated, and tied into knots. The same way he felt every time Diana bested him in their years long battle for the upper hand.

Diamonds. Chocolate. The deed to his house, their home. A darkened hotel room lit only by candles. And yes, he did catch the scent of exotic flowers along with it all. The same scent as Diana's perfume.

He dropped his arms, lowering the box of chocolates and the one containing the necklace with them. It all made sense now. Every last bit of it down to the figure swathed in black, standing in the doorway to the bedroom.

"Why, you little minx," he said as the truth of things hit him square in the chest, causing his heart to soar. God, he loved her. "You little cheat. You had me completely fooled."

CHAPTER 10

*D*iana burst into laughter, unable to contain it for a moment longer. John had looked so alarmed, so panicked when he'd entered the hotel room, but finally, he'd put all of the pieces of her ruse together. The transformation from desperate man, ready to do anything for his wife, to bested man, ready to do anything *to* his wife was too much for Diana to endure without doubling over in laughter.

"Your face, John," she said, peeling back the hood of her cloak and revealing that, yes, she was the mysterious person he had been dealing with all along. "Your face is absolutely priceless at this moment."

"You blasted woman," John growled, throwing the two boxes he carried—like a suitor coming to woo his bride, whether he realized it or not—onto the nearby sofa. He strode across the room with purposeful strides. When he reached Diana, he grabbed her arms with a grip that was almost bruising. "You incorrigible harridan. You had me frightened out of my wits for your safety." His eyes glowed with ferocity, but it was far more passionate than violent.

"Now, now, John." Diana stared back at him with an impish smirk. "You had yourself frightened out of your wits. If you'd had any wits to begin with, you would have noticed all of the glaringly obvious hints I left throughout this entire charade."

John blinked at her. He took a half step back, still holding her arms, confusion creasing his brow. "What hints?"

"All of the times I asked you about your finances, for one," she said, arching one eyebrow at him.

"That was...I didn't...." He shook his head. "I don't see how that counts as a hint toward you staging your own kidnapping." He narrowed his eyes and tilted his head to one side. "Did you do all of this merely to draw me to a hotel room where you could seduce me?"

Diana's jaw dropped. She didn't know whether to continue to be angry with John for his bullheadedness or to laugh at him for still behaving like a fool. "You believe this is all about me luring you to a hotel?"

"We don't have time for this." He stepped back, shaking his head. "I'm being chased by members of the underworld. They could be here at any moment with murderous intent. Come along, we have to get out of here." He grabbed her hand and yanked her toward the door.

Diana yelped as she was tugged forward. Her cloak slipped off her shoulders, revealing the other part of her plan. Beneath the cloak, she wore nothing more than a rather diaphanous nightgown that she'd purchased from a French lingerie catalog. It left very little to the imagination, and at that moment, John was pulling her toward the door.

"John, you daft fool, I cannot leave the hotel room in my current state," she said, trying to tug on his arm.

"Oh, but you must," he said, glancing over his shoulder at her with a serious frown. "The man who holds my debt could be here at any moment with a dozen armed men to murder us like dogs. We must escape this very instant." He pulled her across the room and reached for the door handle.

"John, no. No! I cannot so much as step out into the hall like this," Diana argued. "My reputation is in shambles already. If I am seen by so much as one person dressed like—"

John glanced over his shoulder at her again, this time with a wicked grin. Diana stopped mid-sentence, her mouth hanging open.

"You bloody bastard," she said yanking her hand out of his and smacking him hard and repeatedly on his arm. "I should have known you were teasing me yet again. You impossible, horrible, devilish—"

She didn't have a chance to finish. John swept into her, clasping her around her waist and kissing her with a force of passion Diana had never known. He molded his mouth to hers, his lips and teeth teasing hers until she opened for him. When he thrust his tongue alongside hers, Diana sighed deeply, throwing her arms over his shoulders. He continued to devour her with energy that was both desperate for her long-awaited surrender and punishing because she'd made him wait so long.

She almost didn't want the kiss to end, wanted to proceed straight to the intended finale of the night, but John pulled back suddenly. He stared deeply into her eyes with a combination of steel and amusement.

"How did you manage to persuade Pratt to go along with your little ruse?" he asked, eyes glittering with curiosity.

"I didn't have to persuade him about anything," Diana answered, hoping her expression was as impish as she felt it was.

"But he told me my debt had been sold." John arched one eyebrow.

"And so it was," Diana announced with a triumphant smile.

"But it couldn't have been. That man—" John stopped. This time, it was his turn to stand stock still, his mouth hanging open, as the pieces of the puzzle fit together in his mind. His gaze lost focus for a moment before snapping keenly back to hers.

"Yes, John. I purchased your debt," she revealed, standing taller and tilting her chin up proudly. "Or rather, I simply paid it off, as I am your wife."

"But you couldn't have." John shook his head. "How would you possibly have managed it?"

Diana let out a long-suffering sigh. "John, really. How many times do I have to tell you that I have been investing successfully for years, that I have great, huge sums of my own, disposable money, and that I was more than capable of alleviating your financial situation right from the beginning, if you had just trusted me?"

John continued to stare at her, as though she were speaking Mandarin.

Diana shook her head and stepped away from him. She walked to the table at the side of the room, picking up her bank book, which she'd left there in anticipation of just such a moment, and returned to him. She silently handed him the book.

John took it with a dubious look. He opened it, still appearing doubtful, scanned the first few pages without being impressed, then made his way to the newer part of the ledger. His eyes widened and his shoulders hitched as he drew in a breath and held it.

Finally, he reached the end, where the record of her repayment of his debt was recorded, and exclaimed, "My God, woman. Where did all this money come from?"

Diana crossed her arms, sending him a teasing look. "I can teach you how to invest wisely, if you'd like. Heaven knows you need tutelage in that area."

John glanced from the book to Diana. His surprise was delicious to look at, but even more satisfying was the look of apology and admiration that replaced it. "I am so sorry," he said, stepping closer to her. He tossed the bank book onto the sofa with the chocolate and necklace boxes, then drew her into his arms. "I feel like a right idiot for letting my prejudices get in the way of recognizing what a wonderful, talented, clever, amazing woman you are."

"Yes, well." Diana slipped her arms over his shoulders and leaned into him, loving the feel of his body against hers at last. "As long as you promise never to repeat your sins, I might be able to find it in my heart to forgive you."

"At this point, I'm not certain I deserve forgiveness," John said with a wry grin.

"I'm not sure you do either," Diana sighed dramatically. "Particularly since we could have been married years ago, if you'd only confided in me sooner." She stole a quick kiss, then said, "But I will forgive you, because you said that I was the most precious thing you have. And after your sad story the other day, I have half a mind to think you were cheated by men with nefarious intentions."

John made a sound of acceptance and leaned in to kiss her, but before their lips met, he pulled back. "Hold on. When did you hear me say all of that?"

Diana laughed deep in her throat. "There was a false bookshelf in the office where you met Mr. Piper the other day."

"Mr. Piper?" John shook his head in confusion.

"The actor I hired to play the role of your new creditor," Diana revealed, her smile growing. "Though I'm shocked that you didn't discover that as the ploy it was far sooner."

John's body went tense against hers as he gaped at her. "How would I have? The man was entirely convincing."

"The letter, you adorable fool," Diana laughed. "Did you not see how it was signed?"

"It was signed with initials only," John argued. "DD —" He stopped as realization dawned in his eyes. "Diana Darrow, Lady Whitlock." He groaned and planted his forehead against hers. "God, I've been such a fool."

"Yes, you have," Diana laughed. "But you've been my fool. And you will continue to be my fool for ages to come."

He inched back enough to look at her, adoration in his eyes. "But what about your ruined reputation?"

"Oh, that." Diana shrugged, though the loss of that reputation still stung. "Society is fickle. Once the next scandal comes along, and once it is revealed how wealthy I have become, thanks to my independent investments, I am quite certain that I will be welcomed back into the circles I wish to be a part of. Even if it is only so that I can teach other ladies to invest wisely at first."

"They would be fools not to accept you with open arms," John said, then closed his mouth over hers in a kiss. Diana was more than ready to give into it, to give in to him, at last. "And I would be an idiot not to repay your forbearance in the most pleasurable way possible right this very minute."

"I was hoping you would say that," Diana said, her breath catching in her lungs.

John made a sound as though he couldn't wait to give her everything she deserved, and with interest. He lifted her into his arms, and she wrapped her legs around his waist. Her heart pounded in expectation as he carried her into the bedroom.

"You planned this entire thing to lead up to this moment, didn't you?" he asked as he laid her across the hotel's large bed.

"Of course, I did, darling," she said, enjoying the sight as John stepped back to begin hurriedly removing his clothes. "I wanted to ensure that you felt so much in my debt that you would treat me to a night of passion I wouldn't soon forget."

John paused halfway through removing his waistcoat. "Diana. You had to have known that I would have made this an astoundingly satisfying experience for you, no matter what."

"I do know that," Diana laughed, sending him a sultry look. "Though I would believe it a bit more if you would hurry up and remove your clothes."

John grinned from ear to ear and rushed to do exactly as she said. Diana bit her lip and watched as he finished with his waistcoat, then tugged his shirt out of his trousers. He dispensed with his tie and peeled his shirt off over his head, revealing that warm expanse of chest that she'd admired so much half a dozen times or more now without letting herself touch. But it was the way he unfastened and stepped out of his trousers that had her pulse racing.

He was magnificent. His strong thighs were powerful and beautiful. But it was the proud, thick length of his cock that excited her beyond belief. She'd waited so long to see him and to touch him, and she wasn't disappointed.

"I'll go slowly and be gentle," John promised as he climbed onto the bed, positioning himself over top of her.

"Don't you dare," she warned him, grasping the sides of his face and yanking him down for a kiss. John tensed in surprise at her eagerness for a moment, then relaxed into the kiss with a deep chuckle. "I've waited too long for this to have you hold back," she finished, panting.

John continued to laugh as he let his hands wander freely over the thin silk of her nightgown. The vibrations as his body touched hers drove Diana wild. "I've waited forever for this too," he said, kissing her lips, her jaw, and her neck. The exploration was divine, but he paused to balance above her. With a devilish look, he said, "Let's remove this admittedly delightful bit of finery so that we can enjoy each other fully."

"Yes, please," Diana sighed.

She helped John along as best she could by wriggling as he tugged at her nightgown. He was able to sweep it up over her head and toss it to the floor quickly, which made Diana gladder than ever that she'd thought to wear such a thing.

Those thoughts were blasted clear out of her mind as John dipped down to kiss her once more. His naked body pressed against the length of hers. It was so simple, and yet it felt so wonderful that Diana moaned in satisfaction. John's torso was so firm and muscular. The hair on his chest was scintillating as it tickled her sensitive breasts. His thighs were every bit as powerful as she'd imagined as they wedged between her own. And the stiff, hot length of his cock against her belly was everything she had ever hoped it would be and more.

"I might never forgive you for making me wait so long for this," she sighed as he shifted his mouth from her lips to her neck and lower.

John chuckled deep in his throat. "You haven't even begun to experience all there is to not forgive me for," he said.

Diana started to laugh, but the sound was cut short as he reached once of her breasts. He kissed and licked her, capturing her nipple in his mouth and tormenting it with his teeth and tongue. Diana gasped at every new sensation he drew from her, threading her fingers through his hair and encouraging him to go on and on. He teased her other breast with his hand, rolling her achingly sensitive nipple between his finger and thumb as his mouth continued to work on her. And then he switched which breast was getting which kind of attention, somehow making everything a thousand times more pleasurable.

When he finally broke away from her, it was to gaze up at her and say, "I love you, Diana." He was short of breath and passion hazed his expression, but Diana felt his words through her whole body. They pulsed in her sex as though he'd touched her. "I have always loved you. And I always will love you."

"And I love you as well," she sighed, aroused by the love in his eyes. "Even if you are a fool."

He laughed, which filled her heart with bliss beyond measure. Then he continued teasing and tormenting her body with pleasure like she'd never imagined was possible. He kissed his way down over her belly, impatience rippling off of him. Her excitement grew with each press of his lips lower and lower on her body, until it reached a towering level as he brushed his hands along her inner thighs, pushing them apart. She felt impossibly exposed to him, on display in the most carnal way imaginable, and she loved it.

"Oh, God, John!" she cried out when he brought his mouth to her sex, exploring her with his lips and tongue. Her whole body felt liquid as he tasted her. The pleasure he gave her was so overpowering that she felt the tell-tale coil of orgasm forming deep within her, even before he moved his mouth to her clitoris.

She made plaintive cries that she'd never heard from herself before as his teasing did its job. Within seconds, her body burst into a cascade of throbbing pleasure like nothing she'd ever felt before. She gave herself fully to it, arching against him and tilting her head back, eyes closed. That was only the beginning, though.

With a deep groan of triumph, John shifted, sliding his body up the length of hers until his lips met hers. He didn't stop there, didn't hesitate for even a moment before guiding his shaft to her still-trembling sex and thrusting inside of her. The momentary shock of invasion gave way quickly to a whole new level of pleasure as he filled her. It felt perfect to have him stretch her and move with commanding purpose inside of her. Even better was the tension in his body and the sounds of abandon that he made as he let himself go.

She'd told him not to hold back, and he didn't. The way he moved in her, taking his pleasure from her as much as she'd taken hers from him, was beautiful. It was everything she'd ever dreamed mating with him would be. Her body felt alive with pleasure, even in the wake of her orgasm, as his cries grew more pitched and his body rippled with need. When he finally tensed with a guttural cry and spilled inside of her, it was as if everything in the world had finally aligned the way it should have.

The aftermath was as good as the moment as well. John sagged against her, spent and heavy, but Diana loved the feeling of his weight on her. She wrapped her arms and legs around him, holding him to her heart. The love that filled and surrounded her was worth every second of the wait to get to that point.

"You are magnificent, John Darrow," she panted, happier than she'd ever been in her life.

"Not as magnificent as you," he laughed, shifting to his side and holding her, even though their bodies were damp with sweat and overheated.

"That's true," Diana told him, one eyebrow arched,

her expression and her heart filled with love. "And don't you ever forget it."

———

I HOPE YOU'VE ENJOYED DIANA AND JOHN'S STORY! And the entire *May Flower* series. This may be the last book in that series, but you can still read about characters that were connected to this book. Like actor Martin Piper, for example. Martin is free-spirited, playful, a little goofy, and gets his own romance as part of my M/M series *The Brotherhood*. Find out what happens when silly Martin is paired with serious and conservative MP Edward Archibald in *Just a Little Madness*.

Or how about John's cousin, Christian Darrow, over in Ireland. Christian is just as much of a prankster as his cousin, and it gets him into all sorts of trouble with Lady Marie O'Shea (yep, that's Fergus O'Shea's sister, who you met in *When Lady Innocent Met Dr. Scandalous*). They have an epic courtship in *I Kissed an Earl (and I Liked It)*, the first book of the *That Wicked O'Shea Family* series!

IF YOU ENJOYED THIS BOOK AND WOULD LIKE TO HEAR more from me, please sign up for my newsletter! When you sign up, you'll get a free, full-length novella, *A Passionate Deception*. Victorian identity theft has never been so exciting in this story of hope, tricks, and starting over. Part of my West Meets East series, *A Passionate Deception* can be read as a stand-alone. Pick up your free copy today by signing up to receive my newsletter (which I only send out when I have a new release)!

Sign up here: http://eepurl.com/cbaVMH

ARE YOU ON SOCIAL MEDIA? I AM! COME AND JOIN the fun on Facebook: http://www.facebook.com/merryfarmerreaders

I'M ALSO A HUGE FAN OF INSTAGRAM AND POST LOTS of original content there: https://www.instagram.com/merryfarmer/

ABOUT THE AUTHOR

I hope you have enjoyed *How to Avoid a Scandal (or Not)*. If you'd like to be the first to learn about when new books in the series come out and more, please sign up for my newsletter here: http://eepurl.com/cbaVMH And remember, Read it, Review it, Share it! For a complete list of works by Merry Farmer with links, please visit http://wp.me/P5ttjb-14F.

Merry Farmer is an award-winning novelist who lives in suburban Philadelphia with her cats, Justine and Peter. She has been writing since she was ten years old and realized one day that she didn't have to wait for the teacher to assign a creative writing project to write something. It was the best day of her life. She then went on to earn not one but two degrees in History so that she would always have something to write about. Her books have reached the Top 100 at Amazon, iBooks, and Barnes & Noble, and have been named finalists in the prestigious RONE and Rom Com Reader's Crown awards.

ACKNOWLEDGMENTS

I owe a huge debt of gratitude to my awesome beta-readers, Caroline Lee and Jolene Stewart, for their suggestions and advice. And double thanks to Julie Tague, for being a truly excellent editor and to Cindy Jackson for being an awesome assistant!

Click here for a complete list of other works by Merry Farmer.

Printed in Dunstable, United Kingdom